RACHEL'S FLOWERS

Rachel Swann takes a sabbatical from her London floristry job to come home and temporarily manage the family plant nursery. But then it emerges that her uncle has also asked the globetrotting plant collector Benjamin Hunter to do the self-same task! Wary of Ben's exotic plans for the establishment, Rachel is determined to keep the nursery running in its traditional manner. But as the two work together, they cannot ignore the seeds of a special relationship slowly blooming between them . . .

CHRISTINA GREEN

---◆---

RACHEL'S FLOWERS

Complete and Unabridged

LINFORD
Leicester

First published in Great Britain in 2015

First Linford Edition
published 2016

A catalogue record for this book is available
from the British Library.

ISBN 978–1–4448–3055–2

Published by
F. A. Thorpe (Publishing)
Anstey, Leicestershire

Set by Words & Graphics Ltd.
Anstey, Leicestershire
Printed and bound in Great Britain by
T. J. International Ltd., Padstow, Cornwall

This book is printed on acid-free paper

1

Sunshine, birds singing, and the old remembered pleasure of being in Devon again. London had been home for the last three years, and it was with reluctance that I was obeying Uncle Dexter's demand that I was needed here; but even so, the magic of the lush countryside and the seeming peace of the small village I drove through were working on my churning mind.

I drove through the winding lanes, remembering pleasures from childhood past; and, as I drew up outside Swann's Nursery, some of the rage I had felt at this autocratic command to come home was leaving me. Yes, Uncle Dexter had a lot of explaining to do, and I would put my point of view very forcibly — no longer was I a child to obey his every word. Even as I pulled my bag from the car, and started walking through the open gate — looking very ruined and in need of repair, I thought — I was planning just what I would say to Uncle Dexter when I found him. Something about women no longer being at the beck and call of men. Didn't he realize that my job in the London floristry business was a good one with exciting prospects? In fact, I would mention all the new attitudes which had been hatched in London and were now talking points among working women.

Smiling to myself, I looked at Swann Cottage, standing at the side of the nursery, and imagined Uncle Dexter's housekeeper, Katie, being as busy as I remembered her. I would see her very soon, but first I must find Uncle in his office.

When I reached it, I stopped in the open doorway, looking inside, expecting to see the great man himself seated at his desk, surrounded by catalogues and books and seemingly lost in thought. But — no Uncle Dexter. Instead, good old Ned Fowler, employed in the nursery surely from the year dot, was sitting there: smiling at me, getting up very slowly, and thrusting out his calloused hand.

'Miss Rachel!'

The Devon burr set my memories going, and I smiled back at his huge, welcoming grin. 'Hallo, Ned — lovely to see you.' I pressed his hand, adding, 'You look the same as ever!'

His grin became a comic grimace. 'Dunno 'bout that, Miss Rachel, years add up, you know. Like your uncle said only last week, when he moved into that place up the road.'

My smile faded. 'Yes, poor Uncle Dexter. Arthritis, isn't it? I remember his old legs playing up when I was here — what, three years ago?'

Ned nodded. 'Says he's gonna have an operation to make them work again — soon, he hopes. But right now, well, 'tis just you and me, Miss Rachel. That is, until the new fella arrives.'

I stared at him. There had been

nothing in Uncle Dexter's letter about a 'new fella'. 'Who are you talking about, Ned? Who is arriving?'

He pulled out a rackety old hard-backed chair, dusted it off, and gestured me to sit before returning to his own seat behind the desk. Tired but bright blue eyes looked at me very directly. 'So Mr Dexter hasn't told you, then? Not about this young chap, son of an old friend of his, who he's asked to help out till he comes back with his new legs? Well, that's what he told me. 'I need a man to run the place,' he said.'

I felt dangerous emotions swirling up inside me. Uncle Dexter had always been autocratic and very much in charge of the family nursery. What he said went. So clearly this was something I was supposed to accept without any argument. 'A man to run the place.' Well! Sharing the work with some unknown young-ster, who would probably have come down from London with his head full of new schemes and ideas? Had Uncle Dexter realized that? And what on earth did he expect me to do about it? Sit down and say *Yes sir, No sir* like a good little girl?

I got up from my hard seat, put down my bag in a dusty corner, and said, as I headed for the door, 'Ned, I'll be back later. I must go and see my uncle straight away. Up the road, you said? What's the address?'

'Fairwater Valley Hotel, lady called Mrs Bond runs it. Give Mr Dexter my best, won't you, Miss Rachel? And I'll have a cuppa ready for when you comes back.'

The hotel looked attractive, a handsome Victorian house with casement windows and a flowering front garden. I rang the bell at the elegant door and was ushered inside by a smiling young girl wearing a floral-patterned tabard. 'I'll go and fetch Mrs Bond,' she said. 'Please sit down . . .' And she disappeared.

As I waited restlessly, I looked around the room. Airy, spacious, with attractive watercolours on the pale walls, and some handsome antique furniture. The armchairs were modern and comfortable, and I found myself thinking that Uncle Dexter could easily have gone somewhere much less his style.

The door opened and Mrs Bond came in: a middle-aged blonde woman with a welcoming smile, but also an air of authority which got me frowning. I stood up and we looked at each other for a long minute. Then, 'Hallo, Miss Swann. Of course, you've come to visit your uncle, who is upstairs in his room. But I thought we might just have a little talk first . . . do sit down.'

I did so, wondering slightly if Uncle Dexter had already blotted his copybook, but then she said quietly: 'It's a pleasure to have Mr Swann with us. A lovely gentleman and we shall look after him to the very best of our ability. But — ' She paused, and I felt myself tense. *Always a but, isn't there?* I thought.

'You see, Miss Swann, he has plans to recover from the operation and then return to the nursery. But this may not happen. I accompanied him to the hospital last week, and heard the consultant

6

giving him advice — about not expecting a full recovery. Perhaps not being able to walk as easily as he was hoping.' She smiled, and I saw sympathy beneath the firm expression.

I took a deep breath. 'I see. And that would disappoint him very badly. If he didn't have the nursery to fill his life, then I'm not sure what he would do . . . '

She nodded, and I knew she understood. After all, running a hotel where hopeful residents were often disappointed at their chances of recovery, she knew all about this sort of thing, and was able to cope with it. But as for me — I was new to the ravages of old age, and what an ailing life might entail. And suddenly I knew Uncle Dexter was the strong force in my life, had been since my mother died when I was still at school, and that I must do everything I could to help him get on with his life — even if it proved difficult.

I smiled very firmly at the woman who was watching me with keen eyes, and said, 'I'm sure that between us we'll help my uncle to cope somehow, Mrs Bond. And now perhaps I may see him, please?'

She rose at once, smiled again, and led me to the door. 'I'll take you to him at once, Miss Swann. I know he'll be delighted to see you, he's been waiting for this moment ever since he first wrote to you.' We paused at a lift shaft, went up a single floor, and then got out in a long passage painted a warm peach colour, and with a comfortable-feeling oatmeal carpet. 'Your uncle has the best room in the house,' Mrs Bond said as we walked the length of the passage, stopping at the last door, on which she knocked gently, and then called out, 'Your niece to see you, Mr Swann. May we come in?'

Uncle Dexter's voice sounded just as I remembered it. Loud, warm, and very decisive. 'Of course, Mrs Bond. Come in, Rachel.' And, just as I used to as a child, I did as he told me and went into his room.

'Uncle! How are you? I do hope you're comfortable here . . . ' I was in his arms, smelling the familiar scent of cigars and a touch of aftershave. He looked well, I thought — perhaps a few extra wrinkles around his penetrating dark eyes, and a little extra flesh around his strong chin, but still handsome. A man you could admire — and, with me feeling my childhood come back, love very deeply. I murmured, 'Good to be back here, Uncle, with you . . . ' and then stepped away, knowing I mustn't let sentiment overwhelm me when there was so much of importance to discuss.

Mrs Bond, in the doorway, said quietly, 'I'll send a tray of tea up, Mr Swann. I'm sure you and your niece would like a cup as you talk.' The door closed, and Uncle Dexter raised one greyish eyebrow.

'Nice woman. Runs the place efficiently. Now, sit you down, Rachel, child. My word, it's wonderful to have you here.'

I retreated to a comfy armchair by

the window and watched as, stiffly, he lowered himself into what was obviously his particular chair. I saw at once that his legs were slow and difficult to control, and it dawned on me that Uncle Dexter was ageing, despite his still-charismatic presence and warmth.

We looked at each other, and he nodded his head, smiling. 'You want to know just what I've got planned, of course, Rachel — so this is it. I get these old legs sorted out — which will take about three to four months, they tell me — and then I'll be back. And in the meantime, you and Ned can do all the usual chores in the nursery, and young Benjamin Hunter will take over the management. Do you agree?'

A knot twisted in my stomach and I sat up straighter. I met his questioning eyes with my own, and somehow managed to try and say what I felt.

'No, Uncle Dexter. I don't agree; not with this business of bringing some chap into the nursery — Benjamin Hunter, you said? — and letting him lord it over us. I mean — what does he do? Is he a businessman? Whatever, he's sure to have new ideas and plans . . . you can't possibly let someone like that loose in our family nursery.'

My words hung in the air as I waited anxiously for his reply. But he just sat there, looking at me, occasionally rubbing his right leg with his hand and frowning. Until, slowly, he said: 'I might have expected all that, Rachel. A headstrong girl like you, leaving what you told me is a very good job in London, and then being expected to work as a labourer for a short time — no, of course, it doesn't please you. But I thought — hoped — that for the sake of the nursery, and our family, that you would forget your scruples and do as I ask.'

I forgot the knot in my stomach. Instead, I was back in childhood, hearing Uncle Dexter reprimand me for some terrible thing I had done — or not done, having forgotten his instructions.

But slowly, as I sat there, staring at him, it dawned on me that I was a child no longer. I was a young woman with experience of the trade I had followed for the last three years. I was able to meet him on his own ground. And so I took a deep breath, and said, as quietly as I could manage: 'I will do all I can for the nursery, Uncle Dexter. You know that; you can trust me to do so. But, as I'm sure you know, the days are gone when women were merely workers while men did the leading. If this Hunter guy comes, then he will have to share the overall management of the nursery with me, until you can return and take it over yourself once again.'

'Hmm,' said Uncle Dexter, and started rubbing the other leg.

A knock at the door, and the girl arrived with our tea-tray. The business of finding tables and getting settled took a little time, and when I finally put Uncle's milkless teacup on his small table, the atmosphere had changed slightly. We smiled at each other, and I offered him the plate of macaroons.

'Yum, almond,' I said, 'and looks like home-baked. Go on, Uncle, treat yourself . . . '

He did so, and returned my smile. By the time we had emptied our cups and I was pouring seconds, his next words were what I hoped for, although I had hardly expected them.

'Seems that young Hunter will meet his match in you, my girl — but there, that's the world today, I understand. So — very well, you shall have your equal position. But both of you must remember it's only for a short while. And when I can walk again and return to the nursery, you can go off and find new jobs. You won't be needed here any longer.'

I said nothing, but remembered what Mrs Bond had warned me about. What if the operation didn't produce the outcome he was relying on? But, wisely, I kept my thoughts to myself. I took another macaroon, saw him do the same, enjoyed the twinkle in his eyes, and finally said, quietly and with uncontrollable amusement in my voice, 'So when does this estimable young man arrive, Uncle? And should I be at the station to welcome him? Or will he drive up in his Porsche? Or even land by helicopter?'

We laughed then, and I felt the years fade away. He would always be the strength in my life, and I would work with Benjamin Hunter if that was what he wanted. He leant forward to transfer the cake to his plate, and said, with a wicked glance at me, 'Don't push me too far, darling girl. Just do what you can, and let events unfold.' And then, before biting into the macaroon, he added quietly, 'I daresay there's a message waiting for you in the nursery. Then you'll know how to greet him. And I've already told Katie in the house to get rooms ready for both of you. All right, then, Rachel?'

'Yes, Uncle,' I said obediently, matching the gleam in his eye with what I felt in my own. 'All right.'

2

I left the Fairwater Valley Hotel, Uncle Dexter kissing me fondly, and saying, 'Bring the young man to see me first thing tomorrow morning, Rachel — we shall have a lot to talk about.'

I said yes, but thought to myself that the talk would, of course, be orders. Well, so be it. Tomorrow was a new day, and I had things to do before it dawned. Like going to Swann Cottage and showing myself to dear Katie, Uncle's housekeeper who had helped bring me up, and then back to the office to see if this young man — Hunt? Hunter? — had left a message telling us when he was due to arrive.

Katie welcomed me with a familiar warm hug and a catch in her quiet voice as she said, 'Oh, Miss Rachel, wonderful to have you home again — I've got a nice supper ready for you in an hour or so — I expect you want to unpack and then look around the nursery, don't you?'

'As usual, Katie, dear, you've thought of everything. Yes, I must have a stroll around, and then I'll be here. I've just seen Uncle Dexter — he seems in good spirits, and so sure that he'll back again before too long . . . '

We looked at each other, and I saw on her face the same uneasiness I felt myself about Uncle's return to the nursery. But we didn't say any more, and I took my bag upstairs to what had always my little room under the eaves, feeling a strange happiness at being here once again.

Unpack? I grinned — I had brought very little with me; just jeans, t-shirts and strong shoes mainly, for I knew what was waiting — hard work and hot temperatures in tunnels and glass-houses. But I carefully hung up the one smart dress which I had added at the last moment — after all, one never knew if there might be a social occasion that would need me to look tidy. Uncle had lots of friends, and perhaps after his operation, there might well be a celebratory meal somewhere . . . At the thought, I smiled and pushed away the previous uneasiness about the results of his operation.

And then, out into the nursery, looking intently at the growth which seemed to fill every bed. I forgot about any possible message from Benjamin as I felt the old happiness returning, bringing an easy smile to my face, and sheer joy into my mind. For the flowers stood tall and beautiful, shrubs leaned over them, and smaller blossoms took their places lower down in the beds, all in perfect condition, and sending that well-remembered fragrance of natural sweetness all around me. How could I be anything but happy and full of hope to be back here, at Swann's Nursery, with the summer growth parading itself before my adoring eyes?

After a long, slow wander around the flower beds, the tunnels and the one big glasshouse, I sighed, knowing it was time to go back to Katie and her meal. I passed the office: shut and locked up now, with Ned homeward bound. But someone was standing outside the door, someone looking impatiently about him, and then coming towards me rapidly as I approached. I knew instantly who it was — this must be young Benjamin Hunter. But he wasn't at all what I been expecting.

I stared, aghast at the untidy, shabby clothes this tall, raggedy-haired man wore; at the shoes which looked as if he had trekked here from some remote fastness, so worn were they, that I wondered how they remained on his large feet. He stared back at me, and then halted at my side, looking down into my astonished face with frowning vivid blue-green eyes.

'I suppose you're Rachel,' he said, and I thought he sounded as if he found my presence unacceptable. His voice was quiet, actually rather attractive, but it was the expression on his suntanned, slightly lived-in face, that caught me, a sort of *So who is this girl and what's she doing here?*, and I felt indignation strike me instantly.

I took a couple of steps away from him and held my head an inch higher. 'Yes, I'm Rachel Swann,' I said sharply. 'And I imagine you must be Benjamin Hunter. My Uncle Dexter has told me you would be coming.'

He nodded, but didn't bother to smile. 'Yes, that's me. Mr Swann said you would be here.'

Again we just stood there and looked at each other. I had no idea what to say next — should I invite him into the cottage to share the meal Katie had prepared? But in those clothes? Those shoes . . .

And then, slowly, he turned away and looked around him. I watched the expression on his face, hoping the charm of the growing world about him might bring a better change of mood. But even as my thoughts ran like this, he was bending down to finger a leaf, to pull apart the soft petals of a flower, and still he didn't smile. Until, turning again, he looked very keenly into my wide eyes, and said, in that soft voice that was almost a whisper but carried like music, 'I think we might make some changes, Rachel — we must have a chat about it. But now — can I go and tidy up? Your Uncle said I was to have a room in his cottage.'

'Yes,' I said, wondering a bit now, and thinking that perhaps first impressions weren't always the right ones. 'But where's your luggage? Did you leave it at the station? I suppose you taxied up from there?'

Now, for the first time a smile appeared. So humour was allowed, I thought, slightly relieved. 'I walked,' he said briefly, 'and the only luggage I have is that bag over there.' He nodded towards the door of the office, and there I saw an ancient and extremely shabby backpack, lying where he must have jettisoned it.

I took in a deep breath, ordering

myself to be polite and not let my outraged feelings show. 'I see,' I said wryly with the beginning of a slight grin. 'Travel light, don't you? A good thing we're not in the centre of London — the villagers won't expect you to dress up. This way. I'll introduce you to Katie, the house-keeper. She's got a meal ready — are you hungry?'

And that's when I understood the old adage *The way to a man's heart is through his stomach.*

Benjamin Hunter produced a smile that was almost handsome, and said casually, 'Starving. Haven't eaten prop-erly since I came down from the mountains in Turkey a couple of days ago. And don't worry, I'll buy some-thing tidy for the village invitations if I have to.'

Invitations? I thought. *I don't imag-ine the vicar or the parish councillors, or the lady of the manor — or, specifically, Uncle Dexter — will be inviting you anywhere. You're here to work, Benjamin Hunter, and I'll make sure that you do.*

I led him towards the cottage, and waited to see clean and hygienic Katie's response to this weird and unmannered visitor.

She amazed me by smiling warmly at him, saying, 'Your room is all ready for you, Mr Hunter, and the water's hot if you would like a bath. And perhaps while you do that, I could brush your shoes for you? Walking picks up such a lot of rubbish, doesn't it?'

I cut in hurriedly. 'But the meal, Katie — don't want to spoil it, do we?'

'No, no, Miss Rachel — a casserole will keep for ages in a warm oven. And perhaps you would like to lay the table while Mr Hunter has his bath?'

Put in my place, I ignored the chuckle that came from Mr Hunter, and said quickly, 'All right, Katie. And you — ' I looked him in the eye and dared him to laugh. ' — come with me, I'll show you your room. And the bathroom . . . '

We met again half an hour later, and

certainly our visitor had done his best to conform to our unsaid requirements. Hair was flattened, lying around his small ears, and hardly touching the clean shirt collar. A brush had been used on the shabby jacket, which now showed leather patches on the elbows; an attractive tweed which, worn as it was, was certainly Harris, or something of equally good quality.

As he came into the kitchen, I saw Katie's face light up. 'I hope you're hungry, Mr Hunter,' she said. 'And that you like devilled chicken?'

He smiled at her, and I heard that voice in my mind whispering, *Maybe he's not so weird as I thought at first. He's quite charming, really.* That idea grew more acceptable as he answered her. 'Sounds like one of my favourites, Katie. Don't worry, I'm ready to do justice to your cooking — you know the old saying *hungry as a hunter*? Well, that's me all right. And by the way, please forget the 'Mr', I'm Ben.'

'Ben?' I was surprised. *But why?* I

wondered. After all, Uncle Dexter had said he was a Benjamin — but perhaps I had imagined that the rather old-fashioned name would bring with it an old-fashioned person. But *Ben*? I felt my smile ease up, and he returned it as we pulled out chairs and sat opposite each other. Looking across the kitchen table, a feeling of growing friendliness helped me ask the question dancing around in my mind.

'I know you've come here to help out for a few months, but what's your normal work, Ben?'

He took a mouthful of the heaped chicken on his plate, savoured it, grinned as he nodded at Katie, and then looked back at me. 'I'm a plant collector,' he said. 'I travel all over the world searching for new, exotic plants — Ben Hunter is a hunter, see?' Then he took another mouthful.

I murmured a foolish 'Oh,' because I didn't know what else to say. His grin broadened as I hastily left the table to find an opened bottle of red wine half-forgotten from yesterday evening. A drink would help us both to communicate, I thought desperately, so I poured him a large glass and finally found words. 'How exciting,' I said, sitting down again, and then knew he must think me a fool. Surely I could say something more intelligent than that?

We sipped our drinks and looked at each other. And slowly his grin eased down into a warm, friendly smile that made me return it. And at last I felt more comfortable. I asked, 'Does Uncle Dexter know you collect plants? Is that why he's having you here, to put weird new specimens into our old nursery?'

Ben took another mouthful and relished it before answering. Then he lifted one of those dark eyebrows, and said, 'I don't know what my father told him, but they're old friends, and I daresay he just wanted a man about the place while he's not here. That's probably it, don't you think?'

I nearly choked over my mouthful of wine. Recovering, I glared at him. 'He might have thought that, but now he's thinking differently — ' I stopped abruptly. *Was he? Had my message of strength really reached him?* I went on, voice rising and quite forgetting the plate of half-eaten chicken in front of me: 'He knows I'm a businesswoman, taking a short sabbatical for a couple of months because of family duty. He knows I can run the place in his absence.'

Ben Hunter's smile died. He stared into my angry eyes for a long moment, and then said, very quietly, something like 'Hmmm,' which made me even angrier. And thank goodness for Katie, who said smoothly, 'Another spoonful of gravy, Mr Hunter? And perhaps another helping of broccoli? I don't want any bits left, you see,' which had the planned result of us passing plates and not speaking for a few minutes, during which I could see him thinking hard and trying to suppress a certain amusement, while I reviewed what I had just said, and was ashamed of how unattractive I must have sounded.

Looking down at our refilled plates, Ben said quietly, 'And what was your business, Rachel? I know you worked somewhere rather important in London.'

I took in a deep, comforting breath and said, equally quietly and not meeting those enquiring, vivid eyes, 'I am a partner in Beautiful Bunches, a growing business in the city which deals with cut flowers, bouquets, installations and arrangements, that sort of thing.'

'Weddings and birthdays? I see. And you've given it up to come here and help Mr Swann out?'

Feeling the old pride in my work return, I was able to look at him, smile, and say easily, 'Of course. The family nursery is very important. And I hope while I'm here to add to my understanding of floristry, so that when Uncle recovers and comes back, I can return to Bunches and add some extra knowledge to our partnership.'

Again, that quiet 'hmmm'. A few seconds, and then, 'Cut flowers? Herbs, perhaps? And, who knows, even the odd exotic leaf or two?' The charming smile broke out again and I felt my own lips curling upwards. He lifted his glass. 'And so we might find we have something in common, after all, Rachel. Shall we drink to that?'

'Why not?' I leant over the table and we touched our glasses before drinking. And it came to me, suddenly, and with a new sense of warmth, that this was a deal which could have lots of potential.

But I was still a bit uneasy about what Uncle Dexter would say when he knew the new helper was more interested in foreign, exotic plants than the family cottage garden flowers we grew here at Swann's Nursery. I caught Katie's eye, smiled at her, and guessed we were both thinking the same — we would just have to wait and see.

3

Before we left the nursery next morning, I picked a tiny posy of spring flowers which I put in a small cut-glass vase Uncle Dexter used to have on his desk, for I guessed he was missing all his blooms.

Ben looked at what I held in my hand, the little sprig of budding daphne and the small primroses and late snow-drops, as we walked up the road to Fairwater Valley Hotel, but he said nothing and I was glad. I felt anxious about Uncle's reaction to this new sort of so-called manager. But, as we walked, I thought a bit harder, and supposed that Ben was, after all, as organized as the next man. He had to arrange his travelling, after all; sort out the plants and seeds he was bringing home . . . it must take quite a bit of organization. So perhaps he knew about managing a business . . . and that

29

made me frown slightly.

Because, of course, I intended to do that myself.

*   *   *

Uncle Dexter sipped his coffee, looked at me over the rim, and I sensed his thoughts. Surprise. Even alarm, perhaps. Quietly, and with a faint smile, as he put down the cup, he looked across at Ben Hunter, and said, 'So — I must be truthful, this is not quite what I was expecting. Your father didn't tell me — plant collecting? Well, how interesting. And where have you been lately?'

I watched Ben's lean face tighten slightly and guessed he was wondering how Uncle Dexter's so-far-easy reactions would continue. But his voice as he answered was steady.

'I've been in Asia, in the mountains, looking for something which would attract my patron, Lord Blanchley. He likes big white flowers and handsome leaves on a tall, upright stem; and, above all, a fantastic fragrance.' His smile grew and he fumbled in a jacket pocket, producing a postcard print of something that was exactly what he had described. 'Like this, the oleander, *Nerium odorum*. And of course, the fact that all parts of the plant are poisonous is another great attraction in one's garden — it will keep the tourists at bay!'

We shared a laugh and I felt great relief at Uncle's big smile. So he wasn't going to start frowning and reducing Ben to a mere nobody who clearly would be useless in his family nursery. I leaned forward, caught his eye and said lightly, 'Perhaps the sort of plant that might stop visitors to our nursery taking cuttings and seeds when they thought we weren't looking, Uncle?'

The laughter grew, and I smiled over at Ben, who, I thought also looked a mite relieved. Abruptly, I wanted Uncle to understand that, in spite of no experience with ordinary garden flowers, here was someone who might well be an asset in widening the scope of the nursery. Strange that I should think that — but then my old thoughts returned: yes, he might well be helpful, but I was the one who was taking over the management of the nursery in Uncle's absence, and they must both realize that.

Mrs Bond came in with a tray of coffee, admired the small vase of flowers on Uncle's table, and gave me a searching look. I smiled back and said casually, 'This is Ben Hunter, Mrs Bond, who is helping me in Uncle's nursery until he recovers from his op.'

They nodded at each other, and then she said, 'I expect you have a lot to talk about. So I'll leave you. Mr Dexter, but let me know when you are free, and we'll have that little drive I was telling you about.' She laughed, adding, 'That is, if you would care to trust my driving.'

Of course, Uncle smiled and said that he had every faith in her talents, and so she left the room with a last smile to

Ben and me. We drank our coffee, and I wondered exactly how we were going to carry on the difficult conversation now. But Uncle surprised me, once he had put aside his empty cup, by looking at Ben with those questioning eyes, and saying politely but directly, 'Well, can you give me some idea of your business capabilities, Mr Hunter? It's why you're here, so I think we should discuss them. What have you got to say?'

I held my tongue, but sat back and watched how Ben would respond to this plain questioning. I thought he would probably make excuses for not being terribly businesslike, but instead he looked at Uncle Dexter with a firm expression on his face, and said, 'I can keep a very careful eye on your business, Mr Swann, until such a time as you get better. You see, although you might not think me a proper business manager, I have learned how to organize foreign workers, how to obtain the results — finding the plants I need, packing them up and transporting them back to England, and then making a comfortable profit on my sales. I don't think you need much more experience than that here in a small nursery, do you?'

Uncle gave me a glance, his eyes gleaming with what I couldn't quite understand — acceptance, or mounting annoyance? I waited uneasily for him to speak. He took a moment or two to marshal his thoughts, and then said, slowly, as if he were searching for words, 'Yes, you certainly appear to have the basics of the knowledge and experience necessary, but there is one thing I should impress on you, Mr Hunter. And that is that our small business is a family concern. It dates back over a hundred years, and is a vital part of our lives — that is, my own, and, so I believe, my niece Rachel's. In the long-ago past it was my great-grandfather who built up the small garden where he lived, and began breeding favourite plants and selling them to interested specialists in the horticultural trade. Slowly, and with much hard work, he and his daughters Georgina and Sophie became well-known, and indeed famous in this part of our country, as reliable nurserymen.'

Abruptly he stopped, and I saw how he continued to look at Ben Hunter. Faded dark eyes locked onto vivid blue-green ones, and I felt the atmosphere becoming charged. I hadn't thought that he would go into old history before actually employing Ben, but of course the nursery was his entire life, and it was right that Ben should learn how it had built up. Perhaps now that Ben realized how important the business was, he might decide to withdraw his offer of help and return to his plant collecting? I waited, and felt my heart starting to beat a little faster.

But all he did was nod his head slowly, and keep silent, allowing Uncle Dexter to continue.

'So, my boy, you will, I hope, understand that it isn't just a temporary business manager I'm looking for, but someone with a heart who loves plants and enjoys hard work.' Another brief pause, and then: 'Is that you, Ben Hunter, I wonder?'

Now I felt very strange, my emotions suddenly bubbling around and hopes and fears mixing up in a chaotic churning. Out of the blue, I knew I wanted Ben to say yes, but felt it was more likely he would take the chance and make a quick exit. After all, being his own boss in Asia and its mountains probably seemed more attractive than this elderly man's demands. I caught my breath and waited.

I saw Uncle Dexter suddenly bend and rub his left leg, his face contorted for a moment, as pain hit. And just as abruptly, I realized exactly what our conversation was about — building a future for the family nursery. Whether Uncle ever returned to run things was a moot point, and I desperately hoped he would be able to do so. But if not, then of course he — and I — needed someone to take his place. A younger, experienced man who might step in and take the business on into the future. I watched the pain subside, saw him lean back and take a deep breath, his eyes fixing again on Ben's face.

Carefully, his features returning to their normal warmth and intensity, he said, 'I think you sound the right man for the job, Ben Hunter. I'll give you two weeks and see how things go. Do you agree to that?'

Ben waited a moment before answering, and I saw his eyes narrow as, slowly, he said, nodding, 'You don't offer me much of a chance, do you, Mr Swann? But I'll take the two weeks, and hope to let you see that I know what I'm talking about. After all, I have come because my father, your old friend, is keen to help out, as I am. So — yes, two weeks and then we'll talk again.'

He stood up, looked down at Uncle Dexter, and I realized from the expression on his face that he was a determined man, someone who would always do his best. A feeling of surprise, and a new warmth, began to run through me; even though he was here in the position I valued for myself, I did so hope Ben Hunter would be what Uncle was looking for.

We left my uncle with a different look about him, a sort of new hope, and I smiled at Ben as we walked back to the nursery.

Perhaps not exactly to my surprise, when we got there, Ben at once went into the office, saying to me, 'I'll have a look at the books before I get down to any real work. I need to know how things are going this year . . . profits are important.'

I knew I must take myself off and find something to work at. I felt an atmosphere was beginning to build up between us, and it wasn't comfortable. When I had come down from London, it had been with the warm feeling that the nursery would go along as usual, with me in charge until Uncle Dexter was better. But now life had taken a new direction, and as I looked around for gloves, a trowel, and a trug for weeds, I knew I must face up to something quite different.

So when a voice called to me, 'Rachel! Rachel Swann!' I got off my knees and looked around me gratefully. A voice I recognized — someone from the past ... Teddy Walters, who had teased me unmercifully at school, and then, almost grown up, taken me to the village dance and kissed me before leaving me at the front door of Swann Cottage. Teddy, whom I had a crush upon many years ago, and who now was surely coming out of the blue to cheer me up and give me some new enjoyment.

I looked at him as he strolled down the path, that famous smile still in good order, and the quick, peremptory voice full of compliments. Stopping at my side he ran a finger down my cheek, and said, 'Still as gorgeous as ever. More, perhaps ... good to see you, Rache. I thought you were leading the high life in London, working with flowers or something . . . so why are you down here?'

Inside me, something relaxed. I pulled off my gloves, dropped them in the laden trug with the weeds, and smiled back at him. 'It's a long story, Teddy. Hang on while I get us a drink, and then we'll sit down and have a chat. White wine OK?'

'Orange juice, please, Rache. On duty, you see . . . ' He stood there, smiling, as I hurriedly returned to the cottage, poured some drinks, and then snatched a moment to glance at myself in the mirror and wish I was dressed more suitably.

Returning to the garden, I found him wandering down the path that led to the bit of waste ground by the coppice of birch trees. I led him to a wooden bench under the shelter of wandering old rosebushes, and we sat down and drank a smiling toast to each other.

'Well?' he said. 'So tell me all about it.'

Which I did. Uncle Dexter, the

summons back to the nursery, and the sabbatical I had taken to do what I could to help out. I didn't mention Ben. 'Your turn, Teddy,' I said smiling at him, 'and what do you mean, you're on duty? Not an undercover copper, are you?'

'A job that might be even easier than the one I've got.' His smile died and he looked at me very seriously. 'Teaching the village children — Headmaster, actually. I'm here on a special project while the kids eat their lunches.' 'He glanced at his watch. 'Can't stay long, but I'll just ask you and see what you think, Rache. Maybe we'll have to ask Mr Swann, but you could give me some idea of whether it's possible or not.'

'Sounds intriguing, Teddy — so ask me . . . '

He looked around at the waste ground, which was thickly green and in need of cutting, and then back at me. 'Could be an ideal site — you see, the kids want to start growing a garden, and there's nothing nearer than your nursery . . . '

Yes, I could see what he meant — all this ground could well be planted with something more interesting and productive. Our local children growing flowers? Vegetables? Why not? I was smiling as I said, 'I don't see why not, Teddy. Uncle Dexter couldn't possibly object to such a good cause — and this bit of land has been derelict for several years. Time it came back into use.'

I watched his expression lighten, and then he was up again, glancing at his watch. 'Time I was back. Great to see you again, Rache, and I'll pop down one evening to talk things over properly. Could we have a meal at the pub, d'you think? Tomorrow? Lots we've got to talk about, I'm sure.'

'Why not? I'd love that, Teddy. OK, so on your way — I'll gather up the glasses . . . '

I was doing just that, smiling to myself, looking forward to renewing this particular old friendship, and watching him quickly walk through the nursery before disappearing. And then, as I walked slowly back from the bench and its mantle of fragrant white roses, Ben Hunter came into view. He halted, looked at me very keenly, noticed the glasses I carried, but made no comment. But he did say something as together we started walking back towards the cottage.

'That bit of waste ground, Rachel — never used, is it? I think it might be just the place to grow one or two of my plants, if Mr Swann agrees. I've been looking at the figures, and it seems to me the nursery could well expand into some new sales. What do you think?'

What did I think? I nearly dropped the glasses as I glared at him, and tried to find words to deal with this unwanted situation.

4

I stumbled. What with wondering what on earth to say, and not drop the glasses, I was out of control. And then I felt his hand on my arm and those vivid eyes looking into mine with concern.

'All right? You missed your footing, I think — here, let me carry those.'

I snatched back the glasses and glared at him. 'No! I can manage. Just a stupid step. Didn't look where I was going . . . ' I marched ahead of him, and went into the cottage kitchen, putting the glasses on the draining board and avoiding Katie's surprised expression as she asked, 'Something wrong, Rachel?'

'No! Of course not. Nothing wrong. Just — brought in the glasses . . . ' I turned, met her eyes, saw amusement in them, and at once thought, *I'm behaving like a child caught out in something naughty — really, Rachel, grow up, can't you?*

And that sensible notion brought me back to reality. I washed my hands under the tap, found the towel and dried them, all without looking round at Ben, who was chatting to Katie. Then, remembering I was a business-woman used to dealing with all sorts of situations, I turned round, smiled at Ben with a big, sophisticated smile, and said, with laughter in my voice, 'Sorry I was so short with you. Always annoying when one slips, and I was afraid of the glasses breaking. Well, now; lunchtime, isn't it? So, what've you got for us today, Katie?'

I slipped into my seat, noticing that he, too, was amused by the whole silly episode. Katie said quietly, bringing her special brand of serenity to the moment, 'A nice fresh salad and a meatloaf. You liked that when you where a child, Rachel.' And I saw, from her expression, that she was remembering other childish scrapes and arguments.

I unfolded my napkin, watched Ben sitting opposite, and said humbly, as she put dishes on the table, 'Yes, Katie. And I shall love it now. Your cooking is always so wonderful. And that reminds me, it's high time we started seeding the summer veg. I must get on with it.' I looked at Ben as I said this, almost as if I were apologizing for snapping at him earlier, and now was ready to discuss business matters.

He looked back at me, and I saw how the amusement had disappeared, replaced with something stronger and more determined. He ladled out some salad after I had helped myself, and said quietly, 'You're right, Rachel, it's high time we talked about various things. After lunch, perhaps, before we get too involved in the work that's waiting?'

'Yes, what a good idea,' I said brightly, but felt unease spread through me. How would we resolve this difference that has so suddenly grown between us — my school garden, or his exotic plants?

I cut a slice of meatloaf, and decided

that all I could do was to suggest we let Uncle Dexter decide. But what if dear Uncle wanted neither of these innovative ideas in his precious nursery?

* * *

In the afternoon, I made a point of going into the office, talking to Ned who was deep in catalogues and order forms, and waiting for Ben to join us. After all, I thought, he had suggested we should talk — so where was he?

Finally, he came in just as Ned was taking himself off to Katie for a cup of tea and I was calling after him, 'Ned, please tell Katie that Ben and I will be later, if she can keep the pot warm.'

A big smile, and I watched Ben slowly settle himself into the big carved chair where Uncle Dexter always sat. I waited for the conversation to start, but he was staring around the room, eyes eventually fixing on a rather grainy old photograph of a family group standing outside underneath the famous blue cedar tree at the far end of the nursery. He got up, walked to the photo, and examined it very carefully before turning to me and asking, 'Your family, is it? The Swanns a long time ago? Quite a big family — any of them left now?'

New thoughts were appearing in my mind, making me also get up and join him in front of the photo. I didn't answer at once because I had no answer, not yet — but I looked at the figures who all stood very erect and well-dressed under the tree, staring at the photographer, and seemingly waiting for his vital black cloth to be removed. And then something inside me asked — *And did they all relax and smile again, and talk to each other? Was it tea-time then? Did they have a tray brought out, and sit under the cedar tree on deck-chairs and have a picnic like we did sometimes?*

Such a strange thought, but one that warmed me inside. One that I'd never had before, in all my life here at the nursery. So why now? Then I remembered that Ben had asked a question. I blinked, cleared my mind. 'Yes, they were probably Uncle Dexter's uncles and aunts, my great-aunts — and weren't those girls pretty? Such elegant clothes . . . I wish I knew who they were. I suppose they were living in Edwardian times — so long ago. So different from now . . . '

'Not really. Just people who loved flowers. Like you. Like your uncle. Like me, come to that.' Beside me, Ben turned and looked at me intently. 'Strange you don't know much about your family. Mine is an open book because my parents are keen on family history. Don't you ever want to know about your aunts in their lovely clothes? And those rather handsome, elegant young men standing with them? If it were me, looking at his old photo, I should be fascinated — want to know more.'

I felt his gaze as if he were looking into my confused mind. Those vivid eyes, that quiet, yet deep, resonant voice making the words sound like music. 'Yes,' I said abruptly. 'You're right. I do want to know. I must ask Uncle, although I don't recall him ever speaking about them. And Ned, and perhaps Katie — they might remember the names.'

'Go and put some chairs under the cedar tree, Rachel — let's do as your family was doing, have tea on a tray, sitting idly about as if work were a dirty word. Won't hurt to take ten minutes off!' And he strode away.

I watched him go up the lawn and disappear into the cottage. Katie would of course provide the all-important tea-tray. What a strange idea of Ben's this was, I thought as I found a couple of dusty deck-chairs in the gazebo which stood in the shadows of the birch coppice a little further down. I dusted the chairs, then sat in one of them; perhaps he thought our talk would be easier if we both sat down in the sun, instead of looking at each other across the office table. And yes, I felt much more relaxed out here, with a thrush singing away somewhere above me, and slow cloud shadows moving over the gleaming green grass. It was quite lovely. I hadn't felt so at ease for a long time, and now the thought of discussing the big question of school flowerbeds or exotic plants from foreign lands filling that small unused plot didn't seem such a difficult thing to talk over. Of course, Uncle Dexter would have to provide the final answer — but how nice to have solved the problem in a friendly way before that.

I was smiling when Ben appeared, carrying a laden tray, and stopped at my side. 'Couldn't manage a table too,' he said, 'but Katie said there might be one in the gazebo. Hang on a minute.' I watched him go into the old building and come out smiling triumphantly, carrying a bamboo table — which must have held all the dust of a thousand years by the look of it; but Ben dusted it off, put the tray on it, and then folded himself into the chair beside me. 'You be mother and pour, Rachel,' he said, 'and I'll start dishing out the cream and jam. Katie's scones are still warm — be prepared for a feast!'

It was indeed a feast, and I felt a quiet, warm atmosphere surrounding us as we ate and drank. We didn't speak until the last crumbs were spilt onto the grass to feed the sparrows, and empty cups refilled. And then I looked at Ben, and knew I had to break the spell.

'There's an idea of providing a few flowerbeds for the local schoolchildren on that patch of waste ground,' I said quietly. 'The headmaster, Teddy Walters, is an old friend, and I'd love to oblige him. After all, lots of schools are into growing flowers and veg, and helping the kids to learn about nature — it would be great to be a part of that in our own village. What do you think, Ben?'

He drank the last of his second cup of tea, and then half turned to look directly at me. 'I agree, of course. And I think your uncle would also approve, don't you? He would see the value of using that small plot of waste land beside the far wall. No ground should remain idle in a nursery like this.' He paused, then continued slowly: 'But as I told you, after looking at this year's accounts, I'm sure he would want to see a financial return, however small, on such a project. And that's why I thought a border of exotic shrubs would fill the bill. They would attract new customers, be a fresh part of our publicity. And my knowledge would let me deal with them.'

I sat back and felt the atmosphere very slowly and subtly change. No more were we newly-met partners, but partners with different ideas and strong thoughts about what we individually wanted. I met his gaze and felt my own face tighten. Sitting up a little straighter in my sagging old chair, I looked away, down the nursery, allowing myself to drift through the summer border and the tunnel where seedlings were being nurtured and sheltered before Easter, when they would be planted out.

Then I thought of what Ben wanted: huge-leafed, giant plants which would swamp out my lovely cottage garden flowers; foreign flowers with waxy, exotic blossoms and strange fragrances. I said, and heard the sharpness in my voice, 'I hope Uncle Dexter will persuade you to try and forget your foreign plants while you're here, Ben — after all, this is an old-fashioned nursery, and I see no reason why it should change.'

I waited uneasily, sure that he would reply in no uncertain terms, putting me in my place. But no, he looked quite relaxed in the chair beside me, and surprised me by saying, 'I understand your reasoning, Rachel. But have you thought about the sort of changes that your family of Swanns must have had to put up with when they all worked here?'

I hadn't expected this. I frowned back at him. 'What on earth are you talking about? I know nothing about my family — except that they apparently all dressed well and elegantly.'

'And had picnics under this ancient tree, just like us. Where, no doubt, they also argued and frowned at each other.' But he was smiling, and so I could do no less than give him a small tight smile in return.

'I don't think that's relevant, Ben. This is now, and that was then — oh, such a long time ago . . .'

He nodded. 'You're right. You're here in jeans and a t-shirt, plus a baseball cap on your head, while your Great-Aunts Georgina and Sophie wore corsets and whalebone and high, tight collars, even when they were working on the flowerbeds.' He grinned at me and suddenly I blazed into a sharp reply:

'That's neither here nor there! You're going off the point — and where on earth did you hear about Georgina and Sophie?'

'You should ask Ned and Katie a few things; they have long memories. Even if you're not interested, it's still true that those two Edwardian ladies worked here in their inconvenient clothes, and — I'm sure of it — argued, just as we are doing.'

I was speechless. This was a Ben I hadn't suspected of having a lively interest in history. But then I thought, *Plants from foreign lands. And of course he knows all the famous Victorian and Edwardian collectors, who were sent out by rich patrons to face dangers and accidents, and native hostility, as well as searching for that one cherished flower that had to come back to England and decorate a big garden. So he does care about history as well as his gigantic foreign plants.*

So I managed a weak smile, and said, in a less-than-determined voice, 'Perhaps you could tell me a few more things about them, Ben? When you have time? Because I think I would very much like to know what sort of woman my Great-Aunt Georgina was.'

He got up, folded his chair, watched

as I too rose, then took both chairs into the gazebo, returning for the table and allowing me to carry the tray back down the sloping lawn to the cottage.

'Come with me to the pub this evening, Rachel, and I'll see what I can do. About seven suit you?'

I nodded as together we walked back towards the office. And then I remembered — I had a date with Teddy. How very awkward! What should I do? I said I had to go indoors for something, leaving Ben looking rather keenly at the waste patch in question, then telephoned the school and had a word with Teddy.

'Hope you didn't expect me at the pub this evening, Teddy? Er — something's cropped up, so perhaps another evening?' A sudden surge of guilt swept through me. It was almost as if Teddy was unimportant to me, but Ben Hunter wasn't — which, of course, was quite ridiculous.

Teddy named another evening for our date, which I agreed with, and we said goodbye. I put my cap back on my head as I went back into the nursery, and found, as I continued my war with weeds, that I was wondering what sort of hats my Great-Aunts wore when gardening. Probably Italian straw and decorated with garden flowers. Yes, I longed to know.

5

I knew I could no longer avoid the discussion that Ben and I must have regarding the use of the plot of waste ground. And we must sort out our different ideas before taking them to Uncle Dexter. But I didn't want to discuss them while we had our meal at the pub — I wanted to enjoy the moment and put work and problems on one side. *Tomorrow*, I thought, as I changed my trousers and top, and glanced in the mirror to make sure I looked more like a businesswoman than a garden labourer.

And when I joined Ben outside the cottage, where he stood surveying the nursery, I knew that I had done a good job. He turned his back on the rows of flowers and shrubs, and looked at me in a way that made little spurts of pleasure run down my back. 'You look — fabulous,' he said. 'I'm privileged to be going out with you, Rachel Swann. Sorry I can't match the elegant clothes . . . but at least I found a clean shirt hidden at the bottom of my bag. Will I do?'

I smiled cheekily. 'Handsome is as handsome does, Ben. And don't let's argue this evening — OK?'

The smile came back at me tenfold. 'OK, Ms Swann. You're the boss.'

We looked at each other, and I thought I definitely had him where I wanted — under my thumb. Until he added: 'For the moment . . .'

My smile disappeared. I turned sharply and said over my shoulder, 'Let's go. I can only spare an hour, and I'm sure you have plenty to do as well.'

He made no answer, and as I walked briskly through the nursery entrance, I thought I heard a laugh — just a small one — which jarred my nerves, and made me wonder if I wouldn't rather be going to a meal in the pub with Teddy instead.

And so, in silence, we walked along

the road until we came to the Bird in Hand, and then I felt the cheerful atmosphere. The warmth of the setting sun, as we sat outside with our drinks, did me a lot of good. And so, looking at Ben, sitting beside me and nursing a tankard of best bitter while I toyed with a glass of white wine, I decided I had behaved rather badly; definitely stupidly. After all, why couldn't Ben and I be friends? We had to work together for a couple of months, and it wasn't as if I had taken a real dislike to him — or him to me, apparently — so, yes, we could be friends. Then, however, something in my mind stirred, and whispered to me: *But make sure he doesn't think you're just a woman, and so can't possibly to run the nursery . . .*

Then I heard him asking a question. And having to repeat it: 'What do you fancy to eat, Rachel? I'll go in and get the menu — back in a minute.'

When he returned with the menu, I had to force my thoughts to relax and to smile nicely at him as I decided I would like the duck breast with various appetizing sauces and vegetables. Because I knew Ben was a man with a strong mind and wouldn't want to work with a spoiled, annoying partner. So I must play my game very carefully.

We ate quietly, both of us relishing the meal, and then, as our plates emptied he looked at me and I smiled back, realizing that I had questions to ask him: interesting facts which, now I thought of him as a friend, I badly wanted to know. 'Ben, tell me about plant hunting. What you do. What do you find? How dangerous is it? And what it's like, working with people who perhaps don't want you to steal their plants?'

He laughed, pushed away his plate and leaned back in his chair. 'That's a lot of information,' he said. 'If I go into all that, we'll be here until after closing time; let me just give you a few facts that'll set up the picture for you. Like having arranged with the local authorities wherever we go that it's OK to take a few seeds, or even a sapling, from their land. No hostility — not nowadays. Of course, it was different in the old days, when collectors were very macho Victorians, and probably armed with guns in case of native problems. And then there were the women — they must have had a hard time.'

I think my mouth dropped open. 'Women?' I asked, unbelieving. 'Surely not — what, with corsets and high necks? With wildlife all over the place — and in hot climates? You're joking!'

'No, Rachel. You need to find out about some of the amazing ladies who went to wild places and painted the beautiful plants they found there. Go up to Kew and look at the gallery of Marianne North's journeying paintings — you'd be amazed. And full of admiration, I guess, too.' He nodded at me, and I found I couldn't take my eyes away from his. He had suddenly come to life: no longer the relaxed man sharing a meal with me, but someone who had a passion, and the knowledge and experience to share it with anyone who was interested. And yes, abruptly I knew I was interested. I wanted to know more.

But he was getting up, saying quickly, 'Can't stay here all evening, can we? I've got some work I'd like to get into — I'll just settle up and then we'll go, OK?' And I was left sitting there, knowing my evening was finished; I must go home while he went back into his own world. All the happy thoughts of how we would work together and make good things happen in the nursery faded away as I rose and pulled my cardie around my shoulders. All right, if that was that, I wasn't going to waste any more time on him. I had work to do, too — something I had been asked to write for a magazine about flower arranging.

I was cool with him when he joined me again, and together we walked back down the lane to the nursery; chatting idly about the evening sky, the bats, how soon the swallows would come this year . . . and then we were back home, outside the cottage, looking at each other rather awkwardly.

I remembered my manners and thanked him for a pleasant meal. 'My turn next time,' I said, but didn't mean it. No, next time I would be with Teddy, and there would be no difficulties between us.

I turned towards the door, but his voice stopped me. 'Rachel, a favour, if you will — I'd like to use the computer for an hour this evening. I know where Ned hides the office key. Is that all right with you?'

I frowned, thinking of the article I wanted to write, but then remembered I had a laptop upstairs in my bedroom. 'Yes,' I said shortly. 'That'll be all right. Just don't fiddle with any of Ned's work, will you? I think he's starting on the autumn catalogue.'

I saw, in the dim shadowy light, how his eyes narrowed, and heard a tone in his voice which told me I was behaving unnecessarily badly. 'Thanks. I'll watch what I do. I'm not a complete novice, you know. Goodnight, Rachel.' And he walked away towards the office.

In the cottage, I had a last nightcap of hot chocolate with Katie, and then went up to my room. I would get to grips with that article about flower arranging — but the words failed to come. Instead, my mind was full of images of women — clad in hot, stuffy, long dresses; painting plants; doing things women never normally did. And I felt my longings to be a superwoman grow and grow, as the pictures filled my mind.

The next morning, we had a delivery of aggregates, and spent ages offloading the sacks and emptying them into the prepared containers. Pebbles were one of my favourite settings for old-fashioned cottage garden flowers, especially around the pond, and as a result I felt very happy out there in the sun, with pleasurable work under my hands. Ben didn't talk much, and I wondered if had annoyed him last night. But when Katie came to the kitchen door and called out that she was making coffee, we halted, left the stones and sacks, and went inside, glad to wash our hands and sit down after all that bending.

'Have you thought any more about the school project?' asked Ben, scooping sugar into his mug.

I paused, uncertain how to reply. Surely he knew I was thinking about it. That I wanted it to go ahead. But something made me wait for the right words to come. And when they did, I was pleased to see his expression change.

'My thoughts, Ben, are that we must go and see my uncle and ask his advice. What about you? Do you agree with that?'

'Yes, I do.' He stirred his mug and took a big mouthful before saying more. But when he did speak again, he was smiling at me: looking vaguely amused, as if I had said something funny, or perhaps unexpected — and that made me wonder if he thought I was a cross-patch sort of woman. So I smiled back when he said quietly, 'If it's OK with you, Rachel, I suggest we go and call on your uncle this afternoon. Before tea. After he's had his nap . . . '

The smile grew, and I giggled as I replied, 'Don't ever say that to him. Uncle Dexter's a man of action, not one to take a snooze after lunch. Yes, I'll be ready about four — there's plenty to do before that. I — er . . . ' I stopped, wondering whether I was being wise in giving orders. But he was looking at me with those intense sea-green eyes, and no sign of any frown, so I ploughed on: 'Actually I could do with a bit of help after lunch if you could manage it; some of the border perennials are badly in need of splitting, and even replant-ing. Do you think . . . ?'

He nodded, got up, took his empty mug to the sink, and then turned towards the door, looking back at me with a grin on his face. 'Yes, ma'am. I'll go and make sure the spade is clean and sharp, if you haven't any more orders for me for the moment.' And disappeared from view.

I was left with half a mug of cooling

coffee, and Katie behind me, saying disapprovingly, 'I don't think he likes being ordered about, Miss Rachel. Men are like that, you know.'

I turned and glared at her. 'Well, if we're to work together until Uncle Dexter comes back, he'll just have to get used to it.'

She went to a cupboard and came back with bags of flour and sugar, looking at me very pointedly as she passed my chair. 'Ways and means, Miss Rachel. Ways and means. Think about that. And now I must make a cake — lemon drizzle, I thought — so if you don't mind clearing the table, I'll just get on with the work.'

Hmm, I thought. *What old-fashioned ideas. Ways and means, indeed! No, what that man needs is to understand that I'm just as good and experienced as he is. Even more so in some ways . . .*

I returned to the pebbles and grit, but Ben didn't appear to help me finish the job. And what sort of work had he been keen to do on the computer last night, anyway? Something to do, no doubt, with those huge exotic plants, which would look foreign and unfriendly in this old-fashioned nursery. No, Uncle Dexter would definitely say no to Ben's idea . . . Not exactly in the best possible mood, I told myself very firmly that I would make sure I got my way with the village school project.

When I took myself off to the summer border, which was certainly badly in need of treatment, I found Ben there, leaning on his spade and glancing at his watch as I appeared. That made me feel even more annoyed, and so I told him what I planned to do. 'The delphiniums must be halved, and the newer bits planted somewhere else. I'll find a space. And then perhaps you would do something with that enormous monarda? I love the scarlet colour of bergamot, but it's too much there, and I want it moved. Again, I'll tell you where . . . '

He didn't reply, just put a hand to his forehead in salute and began digging. We worked for some time in silence.

When he'd completed the delphinium-replanting, and was about to tackle the bergamot, I paused, wiped my forehead with my hand, and said, 'We've done good work, thank you. But now I think we'll leave it — perhaps tomorrow we can do a bit more. Haven't forgotten, have you, that we're going to see my uncle this afternoon? Before tea — which I suppose is about now.'

He looked at me very directly, picked up his spade, started wheeling the barrow of weeds and unwanted bits towards the compost heaps at the far side of the nursery, and said, over his shoulder,

'Yes, ma'am. Which means I've just about got enough time to clean up. See you in five minutes, OK?'

I didn't appreciate the supposed humour, so just said sharply, 'Yes, quite OK,' and watched him as he disappeared down the path, wondering if we would ever be able to work together more amicably.

And so, as I slowly went indoors to clean myself up ready for the visit to see Uncle, I was in a very domineering mood.

6

I heard voices in Uncle Dexter's room as we walked along the corridor towards his door, and wondered who might be visiting him — someone from the village, no doubt. Someone who might remember me, which would mean a gossipy bit of conversation before Ben and I set out our varying thoughts about the waste patch of land in the nursery. I knocked at the door, the voices ceased, and Mrs Bond opened it, looking, I thought, surprised to see us. But the expression quickly changed.

'Come in,' she said, 'your uncle and I were just having a chat — I'll leave you now, and you can have him to yourself.' She disappeared, and Ben and I, exchanging glances, entered the room and closed the door behind us.

'Hallo,' said Uncle Dexter — rather too heartily, I thought, but his smile was warm and he waved us towards chairs facing his. 'So, what's this all about? A deputation to discuss business matters?' But he was clearly glad to see us, and I felt the atmosphere settling down into easy friendliness. I decided to get my ideas in before Ben had a chance to speak about his.

'A wonderful opportunity has cropped up, Uncle,' I said; 'the village school would like to have a bit of our nursery land so that they can grow their own garden. As you know, I'm sure, most schools are doing this nowadays. Teddy Walters — remember him, do you? — is the present headmaster and he called to see me yesterday.' I was about to go on reminding him of the barren patch of waste land which would be idea for the project, when he cut in with a rather wicked smile.

'Yes, indeed, I remember Teddy Walters. Quite a couple, weren't you, once? I seem to recall certain evening dates when you weren't home by the time I had set . . . '

I couldn't believe what he was saying.

I took in a very deep breath and avoided looking in Ben's direction, because I guessed he would be grinning — I *knew* he would be! Sharply, I said, looking at Uncle's dancing eyes and willing him to stop talking about my past, 'Yes, well, that's all done with now. The thing is, I need your approval before I actually get the schoolchildren in and supervise their gardening activities.' I sat back, straightened my spine and awaited his decision.

But it wasn't quite what I expected. He fidgeted in his chair for a moment, moving his legs painfully and grimacing as he did so; once settled again, however, he looked towards Ben. 'I imagine that there is a reason for your presence here with Rachel. Care to tell me about it?'

Ben shot a glance at me and I frowned. But he said, with quiet control, 'Yes, Mr Swann. There is a very good reason why I'm here. Rachel has decided that the village school should use a certain small patch of waste ground, but I have other ideas. You see, I'm thinking of financial profit, as well as added publicity for our catalogues and brochures. I don't think a small village school garden would produce anything like a new border of exotic, even rare, foreign plants — which would expand the boundaries of your nursery, as well as adding new visitors and extra profit. I could organize this new bed, if you approve, and have it on full display within months — ready for the summer visitors.'

A silence crept around the room, and I heard my heart pumping away. How dare he? *How dare he?* After all, the Swann Nursery meant nothing to him: it was simply a short job which he would forget as soon as he was off on his travels again, and I would be left with new gigantic plants which probably needed more experience and information than I could give them; saddled with the overwhelming new responsibility . . .

I glared at Ben, but he was looking at Uncle Dexter, who was saying nothing, but thinking all the more. I watched the expression on his lined face and saw deep thoughts: pros and cons being weighed; the need for a decision . . . and then, slowly, I saw him make the choice.

'My dear boy,' he said smoothly, 'you have the makings of an excellent businessman, and I'm delighted that you are here, running my nursery for me — '

Another terrible silence, which I broke very rapidly, saying sharply, 'He's not running it by himself — we're doing it together, Uncle.'

He responded very quickly, looking at me as if I had been caught in a wicked teenage deed. 'No need to make a big issue of this, Rachel. As I see it, both ideas are excellent. Now, all we need to do is decide just where the different plantings will take place. Yes, the waste patch at the bottom of the garden would do splendidly for Ben's jungle plants . . . but how about establishing the school garden on the patch just inside the nursery entrance? Full of old shrubs at the moment, but could be an eye-catcher if you let the kids grow nasturtiums and marigolds — and even some giant sun-flowers up the gatepost — don't you think?'

I caught my breath and didn't answer at once; but slowly I realized how sharp his mind was, and that his idea was an excellent one. So I said, 'Well, Uncle, that's great. We'll take out the old shrubs and I'll get Teddy to talk to the children. And then I'll help them plan it all out.'

Then I looked at Ben, who said — quietly, in that lovely voice that always seemed so calm and understanding, even when he said things I didn't want to hear — 'Thank you, Mr Swann. So now Rachel and I will get on with the two new beds. I'll see what plants I can beg, borrow or steal from the various gardens I've brought new specimens to — someone will be glad, I'm sure, to thin out the over-growing ones.' His smile was warm and enthusiastic, and I saw Uncle Dexter nod in agreement. He added, 'We'll have an exotic addition to your nursery ready in time for the summer visitors — and for when you return with your new legs, sir.'

We all laughed a bit at that, but I saw how Uncle's approving expression tightened, and guessed the idea of his operation was a bit challenging. And when he said slowly, 'I think it won't be long now until I hear from the hospital about my pre-op assessment date,' I jumped in at once. 'Let me know, and of course I'll take you there, Uncle.'

A moment's silence, and then he said, very quietly, 'Thank you, Rachel, but that won't be necessary. Mrs Bond has already said she will take me — and bring me back again.'

I thought quickly, then said, 'But she's so busy, with this place to run — do tell her that I'll willingly drive you . . . ' His expression changed at once, and he gave me the determined smile that I remembered from childhood.

'I shouldn't worry about that, Rachel. She said it would be a pleasure to take me.'

'I see.' But I didn't. Mrs Bond seemed

to be the one who spent more time with him than I did, and that made me feel guilty. So I smiled, murmuring something about popping in whenever I could, and that I would bring him some flowers from his favourite spring border.

Clearly the visit was at an end. Ben and I stood up, I kissed Uncle's cheek, and with some final vague words of goodbye, we left the room, going downstairs in a silence that continued all the way back to the nursery.

But, as we went through the entrance, Ben put a hand on my arm and made me halt, looking at him and wondering what he wanted.

'I hope we can do both the things your uncle has approved, Rachel. And without any feelings of annoyance or disapproval. You can contact your headmaster friend and get on with organizing the kids, while I take a trip to a few of the gardens I have in mind. And then, if I can bring back some plants, I'll get that waste patch sorted and planted.'

My mind was running riot. He was

telling me what to do — taking charge, being more of the nursery manager than I wanted him to be. I flicked his hand off my arm and looked into those vivid eyes with a directness that I hoped would tell him, without any words, just how I felt.

'Of course, Ben. You must do whatever you have to, and I will get on with my ideas. Actually, I'm seeing Teddy Walters this evening, so we can make a good start while you're away.'

We continued walking until we stopped at the office door. 'I'll tell Ned what I'm doing,' he said, and I heard a new, curt note in those few words.

'Yes, do. And now I'm going to get on with sowing the summer lettuce.'

I left him still looking at me, and felt I had managed to have the last word, despite his obvious claim to be in charge. But as I started in on my task, in the hot tunnel, with perspiration running down my face, the feelings inside me were slowly changing. I was worried about Uncle, and Mrs Bond's seeming claim on him; I disliked the fact that Ben had got his own way about the exotic plants; and, strangely, a slight feeling of excitement was growing as I thought of meeting Teddy this evening. Would our old relationship still be there, growing steadily into something new? As I planted the tiny seeds, I smiled to myself.

When the hot afternoon ended, with the last customer smiling back at me as she left, I turned my thoughts to the evening ahead of me. In the kitchen, Katie asked if I would be in for supper, and I said vaguely that I didn't think so. Gossip in a small village has a way of becoming troublesome, as I well remembered, and I didn't want anyone to imagine that Teddy and I were an item again — at least, not for the moment, although who knew what the future might bring? So I went upstairs with a big smile on my face and a warm feeling enveloping me.

I had no idea what Ben might do this evening — probably phone some of his contacts about the exotic plants. Well, good for him. I was going to live my life, and he could live his.

Newly-showered, hair gleaming, wearing a fresh shirt and some rather splendid brightly-printed pants, and with a good feeling of energy inside me, I left the nursery and walked down to the Bird in Hand. Birds sang, people in their gardens looked and smiled at me as I passed — and, yes, there was Teddy, waiting for me outside the pub. How nice life was, I thought; and gave him a really warm smile in return as we met.

'Rachel, what a treat to see you.' His voice was different from Ben's — louder and more rapid — but easy on the ear, and welcoming. 'Sit down, won't you — tell me what you'd like to drink, and I'll bring them out here where we can watch the sun go down.'

Always romantic, was Teddy, as I recalled. Such things as sunsets and favourite poetry quotations were part of his life. *Part of his courting practices, too!* I thought, grinning to myself. Well, I wouldn't be averse to being courted in a nice, gentle way, would I? My last partner in London, who had left me several months ago, had been just the opposite: quick, loud, too busy for much loving. I had missed Euan badly when he left, but somehow he was just a memory now. And I wasn't in a hurry to find someone else — although, sitting here in the sun, knowing Teddy would be beside me in a minute, both of us remembering happy days of years flown by, I did wonder whether I wasn't becoming just a little sentimental myself. And maybe even romantic?

So when Teddy came out with a tray of drinks and a menu, I pushed aside the soft thoughts, reminding myself that I was here on a project. I was a businesswoman with details to discuss and put into action. We talked over our meal, and I understood that Teddy, as a headmaster, thought very warmly about the children in his care, which endeared him to me. And so, before the glasses emptied and the plates were put to one side, we had more or less decided just where the new garden should be, what shape would be best, and when we would start to work on it.

'I can't wait,' I said happily, and he took my arm, drawing me closer as he smiled.

'You and me together, Rache — like it used to be. I shall enjoy every moment of making this garden. And we must have another evening like this . . . '

We talked even more as we walked back towards the nursery. But as he left me at the nursery entrance — with a peck on my cheek, and a smile that reminded me of the past — I had a sudden change of thoughts. Yes, the school garden was going to be fun, and we would follow Uncle Dexter's ideas; but before then, there was something I had casually put out of my mind. The commission from the gardening magazine asking for a feature on flower arranging. I couldn't put it off any longer; before I went to bed, I must draft out a few paragraphs, then get up early in the morning and type the finished article out. Whilst in the easy pleasure of being here at

Swann Nursery, I had put my career on hold — but that didn't mean I could forget everything I had so far learned about the craft of making eye-catching arrangements, not to mention selling them. Getting into bed, I set my alarm for six thirty.

7

I was up with the lark — and, with a relaxed mind, enjoyed writing up my piece for the magazine. I advised readers to love their flowers, to give them water and care, and to match the container carefully with the chosen blooms. Then, dressed and pleased with what I had achieved, I went out into the garden to make up an arrangement which I could photograph for the magazine.

It was too early in March for the sort of sophisticated flowers which I had used in London in Beautiful Blossoms — lilies and roses and irises; all of them imported, of course — but here in Swann's Nursery were cottage garden plants growing, ready to bloom in the summer and to provide lovely, home-grown bunches.

I wandered around the flower beds and discovered that the almond tree was covered in small, elegant, pink flowers. I cut a straight branch with several deeply-flowered side-shoots, then an armful of big yellow daffodils, which looked even more spectacular with a few white narcissus flowers among them. And then a purple hellebore. All together, they made such a wonderful variety of colours, I decided I needed only a few small primroses around the stems to deepen their impact. From one of the huge green shrubs, already sending out fresh leaves, I cut just a few to provide a little collar for the flowers to rest on where they entered the container.

Now — the container? I walked back to the tunnel where all the work of the nursery went on — seeding, taking cuttings, and so on — and found a well-shaped, small, silvery bucket which would be just right for my little bunch. Water, a handful of flower-food . . . I stood back and nodded my head. Now for the photograph; I could send my article and the picture later in the morning. And then it struck me that I would take this arrangement down to Uncle Dexter in case he needed cheering up. It couldn't be much fun waiting for an operation, could it?

Back at the cottage, I went into the kitchen, and bumped into Ben Hunter coming out. Our eyes met, and we both stepped back. 'Sorry,' we said together, and then grinned foolishly.

'You're an early bird, Rachel.'

I nodded. 'A commission to finish; and then I had to make the arrangement and photograph it.' I moved away towards the table and the coffee-pot standing there, next to an empty plate awaiting its fill of porridge. Yes, I was hungry after my early start.

'Sounds good. Where is it?' he asked, and without thinking, I said, 'In the tunnel. I'll take it up to Uncle Dexter later.'

He nodded. 'Had my breakfast — but I left you a bit of porridge. I'm off to the station. Gardens to see, plants to pick up . . . ' And then he was gone.

Katie and I looked at each other and shook our heads. 'A man with a mission,' she said dismissively, standing with the toast-rack in her hands and waiting for me to sit down. 'And do you fancy fish for your lunch today, Miss Rachel?'

'Lovely,' I said, before tucking into my porridge. 'With chips, please, Katie.'

* * *

I was busy working at removing the big old shrubs behind the nursery gate when a little boy appeared. 'Mr Walters says, can we come tomorrow morning? At ten o'clock, he said.'

I stood up, easing my bent back and smiled at this small, self-consciously important person. 'Right,' I said. 'Tell him I'll be waiting for you all. And let's hope it won't rain. Don't want to plant the garden on a wet day, do we? Are you excited about it all?'

He jumped up and down for a few seconds, and his grin was like the rising sun. 'Yes, yes!' he crowed. 'And I'm going to put in runner beans. I like runner beans. They taste really good.'

'Runner beans will need a sort of fence to grow up. Do you think you can make one?'

'I'll ask my dad for some bamboo sticks; he's got a lot in his shed. Yes, I can make one.'

'Perhaps I can help you?' I offered, enjoying this lively conversation.

He looked at me very straight. 'I don't think you'd be strong enough. Building fences is for men.'

Amused, I nodded solemnly. 'OK, so I'll let you do it. What's your name, by the way?'

Again, that straight stare. 'I'm Gareth Preston. We live down by the station. I've got a sister, Nina, but she doesn't know anything about gardening like I do. You'll probably have to help her.'

'I will,' I said firmly. 'And now you must go back to school and tell Mr Walters that I'm looking forward to seeing you all tomorrow. Ten o'clock sharp, OK, Gareth?'

He turned away, but looked over his

shoulder and flashed me that handsome grin. 'OK, Miss. G'bye!' Then he raced away down the road, leaving me feeling pleased with the way this little project was going. As I returned to digging out shrubs, I thought that Uncle, too, would be delighted to hear this latest news from young Gareth. I must tell Ben, as well — I knew he'd be amused at the promise of this extra male expertise we must expect . . . And then my smile faded. Ben was probably on the train by now, and for a moment I thought, *What a pity; I would love to see his smile as I told him about Gareth.*

Then I stood upright, leaning on the spade, catching a breath as the strange thought ran around my mind. *I was missing him, wasn't I?*

Mid-morning, and Ned came out with mugs of tea. He looked at what I'd done so far, and then shook his head. 'No work for a woman, all that digging out,' he grunted. 'Let me finish it for you — there's other things you can get on with, Miss Rachel.'

I supposed that it was kind of him, but it was as if he was telling me I wasn't any good at the job — which, of course, was infuriating, and I would tell him so . . . But then the words silenced themselves as I stood up straight, smiled at him, rubbed my back, and drank my tea. 'Thanks, Ned. Yes, I've got other things to do — so I'll leave you to finish this off! And then it'll be all ready for the school children who are coming tomorrow morning . . . '

Ned took a deep breath and made a face of being not-quite-happy about something. 'All those kids running about and screaming . . . ' he muttered, but his grin told me he would actually enjoy it when it happened.

'Don't worry,' I said cheerily. 'Mr Walters and I will keep them under control.'

He spat on his hands, rubbed them together, picked up the spade and bent to get on with the digging. But then he looked up at me and grinned. 'You and Teddy Walters, eh? Just like it was?'

'No,' I said very quickly, and began to walk away.

His voice followed me. 'Sorry, Miss Rachel, just remembering things.'

I turned, fixed him with a sharp look, and called back, 'Well, it's time to forget them now, Ned. Please.' And went into the tunnel, where the beauty of my flower arrangement calmed me down, and returned my thoughts to the next thing to do — which was to deliver it to Uncle Dexter.

I washed my hands, brushed my hair, cleared some clinging earth from my jeans, and put the arrangement into a box which I could carry easily up the short distance to the hotel. The girl answering the door smiled as she looked at the flowers. 'Oh, how lovely,' she breathed. 'For Mr Swann, is it? He'll be so pleased — he seems to be a bit down this morning.'

In Uncle Dexter's room, I put the arrangement on the table close to where he was sitting by the window, then bent and kissed him. 'Morning, Uncle. How are you today?'

He managed a smile, not so bright as usual, but his voice had a cheery note in it. 'All the better for seeing you, Rachel, my dear. And the flowers — quite beautiful. One of your own creations, I take it?'

I pulled my chair closer to him. 'Yes, something I'm writing about in one of the flower-arranging magazines. Glad you like it. The almond is beautiful, isn't it? A real touch of spring.'

'Just what I need to cheer me up. This operation, you see — well, I can't be sure, can I, that it will be the success I'm hoping for?'

I took in a big breath. I understood, of course I did, but the important thing was to keep his optimism high. So I said simply, 'We can only hope, Uncle. And I'll always be available to push you around the nursery afterwards — until your legs start to work properly, if necessary — imagine us, wheeling around together! And please try and keep cheerful.'

He gave me one of his loving smiles,

leaned across and patted my hand. 'A lovely thought, dear child, but you must remember you have your career to return to — and so the nursery must jog along without you, whether I'm there or not.'

For a moment, I thought of Ben — if I returned to London and Beautiful Bunches, would Ben stay on at the nursery? Or would he go off on one of his collecting exploits? And, if so, who would help Uncle, good legs or not . . . ?

But then there was a knock on the door, Uncle said 'Come in!' and Mrs Bond appeared.

'Oh,' she said with a wide smile. 'So sorry to interrupt — but just checking with Mr Swann that he will be ready for his appointment at the hospital this afternoon. We'll leave here at two o'clock, and that'll be plenty of time to get you out of the car and into the clinic . . . '

A small, rapid thought told me that *I* should be driving him, not Mrs Bond. But obviously it was all arranged; and if

Uncle Dexter was happy with the plans, then that was all that mattered. I smiled at her, and kept my mouth shut.

I watched her look at the arrangement and saw the smile on her face grow as she said, 'This is beautiful! Is it your work, Ms Swann? I know your uncle said you worked with flowers . . . '

Pleasure spread through me. 'Thank you, Mrs Bond. Yes, I do arrangements, all sorts of things for people — bunches, posies, even instalments on walls . . . ' We shared a chuckle, and then she said, 'Well, you're very talented. And I can't help wondering if your work wouldn't appeal to certain people in the village. I mean, Mrs Haworth Jones at the Manor, for instance. She often has meetings and parties — and I know she buys flowers in town on those occasions, but surely she would prefer to use a local supplier? Why don't you call on her? Take her an example of what you can do . . . '

Uncle Dexter was smiling at me. 'Good advice, Rachel. I think you should follow it up.'

Of course the compliments pleased me. But then I remembered that I was here in Devon for a purpose — and not to further my personal career. Work at the nursery was far more important than that. So I just nodded, murmured that I would think about it, and then asked Uncle Dexter if he needed anything. Could I perhaps get him any newspapers or books when I was in town . . . ?

Mrs Bond was quick to reply for him. 'We have all those things here, so he has them every day. I can get him anything he requires — you must be so busy in the nursery, so you can be sure that your uncle is well-looked-after . . . ' She turned to Uncle Dexter. 'We'll leave about two, Mr Swann, which will give you time to have your lunch and then a little rest. I'll be up here to collect you in good time.' Another turn to look at me, and that wide smile again. 'So nice to see you, Ms Swann — and I do hope the flower idea will blossom!' A laugh, a swish of the pretty skirt, and the door closed behind her.

I looked at my uncle, who in turn regarded me with one dark eyebrow raised. 'A kind lady,' was all he said, but I felt that other remarks remained in his mind. Yes, she was kind — *but pushy*, I thought as I kissed him goodbye, wishing him luck with the assessment this afternoon, and promising I would be along again in another day or so.

Then I remembered Gareth and the school garden. At the door, I looked back at my uncle. 'The school project starts tomorrow. I'll take some photos, and then you can see how it's going. But I think it's going to be an absolute winner . . . Cheerio!'

Back at the nursery, I inspected Ned's work with the old shrubs and was glad to see the site was clear, nicely dug over and even spread with some of the compost we always kept going at the back of the tunnel. Ned saw me there, and came over from where he was splitting some perennials that needed replanting. 'All ready for them, Miss Rachel,' he said, grinning.

'Thank you, Ned; you've done a good job. Yes, the kids will have no problems planting in this nice fine soil. And have we got some seeds of giant sunflowers, I wonder? Uncle Dexter suggested growing them up the gate-posts.'

'I'll see if I can find any.' He turned back to his work.

I went into the kitchen where Katie was frying chips. 'Hungry?' she asked, and I thought, *Yes, I am.* It had been a good day so far. The magazine article; arranging the flowers; seeing Uncle; thinking about Mrs Bond's surprising advice . . . and now, as I sat down to fillet of plaice and those lovely crisp chips, I was busy with ideas for the school garden tomorrow. Sunflowers, nasturtiums, some flowering polyanthus — all things that grew quickly, and would please impatient children. Then Gareth and his bean sticks . . . As I finished my lunch, I had a sort of new thought. How easy it was to do nice things and be happy. Here at the nursery, I had none of the stresses and strains of working in London: wondering if ordered flowers would deliver on time; whether customers would approve of what I was making them; having to catch buses and travel through crowds of people every day . . .

And, of course, that brought Ben into my mind. All those lonely expeditions, away from the world and its often-difficult inhabitants, among the most beautiful flowers and plants. He must have the same thoughts that I did. But he wasn't here, so I couldn't talk to him about them.

I left the kitchen after thanking Katie for the excellent meal, and took myself off to the gazebo at the far end of the busy nursery. I sat there for a lazy twenty minutes, knowing I should really be back there, dealing with customers, and then finally took myself to the tunnel where seedlings needed to be pricked out ready for planting.

I went to bed that night with my head full of sunflowers climbing up the gateposts, and was up bright and early the next morning. This, I knew, was going to be a really good day.

8

They arrived at ten o'clock sharp, Teddy Walters leading the way and a teacher, Miss Thorpe, at the back of the small group of children. I welcomed them at the gate, and was introduced to Miss Thorpe.

'Do call me Bryony,' she said, smiling widely, and with a sideways glance at Teddy — who, I thought, looked slightly alarmed. I reckoned she was a good teacher, amiable but controlled with the excited children . . . but perhaps smiling a little too much at her headmaster.

Ned appeared from the office, carrying four long stakes and a ball of twine. He looked at the staring faces and said firmly, 'Got to make a good shape before we start planting. Agreed?'

There was a small hum of yeses, and then Bryony took it upon herself to carry out his idea. She handed the stakes around, found scissors in her bag, and then told Gareth to start tying twine to each stake in turn. 'And that will make a good shape for our garden,' she said, looking around. 'Can anyone tell me what the shape is?'

For a second no one spoke, and then a small girl with frizzy red hair raised her hand. 'It's a rectangle, Miss,' she said, and everyone grinned. Gareth turned from his twine-tying, frowned at her, and then at me. 'She's Nina, my sister,' he said. 'Only knows things like that, nothing about gardening.'

I gave the little girl a particularly encouraging smile. 'That's marvellous, Nina! Makes a really good start to the garden.'

What a morning that was! They only had an hour, but in that time the shape was made, and the soil felt and assessed and learned about. Then Ned opened the packet of seeds in his hand, and said, 'Sunflowers. You can each plant one — now, let's get them in the right places.' He moved towards the two ancient gateposts. 'Anyone tell me what sunflowers are good for?'

There was a bevy of answers. 'Bees, birds, butterflies — and the seeds taste nice, too!'

I watched the grin on Ned's tanned face grow into a hearty laugh, before he handed out the seeds, found a trowel, and supervised each child planting a seed below the gateposts. *Quite a wonderful moment*, I thought, and was so pleased with myself — and Uncle Dexter's approval of the idea — that I just stood there and smiled at the happy, noisy scene. Then I went and fetched two watering cans which were put to good use.

When their time was up, Ned and I said goodbye to everybody, saying we'd see them next week — perhaps the seeds might be up by then, and they must all think about the garden and look forward to the next thing we do with it.

I watched them straggle down the road, chatting and laughing, and then heard the telephone ring in the office. A customer? I felt a sudden sense of fear — not bad news about Uncle, surely?

But it was Ben's quiet voice that came down the wire. 'Rachel? Morning. I've got some interesting news for you, if you've a moment to spare.'

'Yes,' I said. 'What is it, Ben?'

'Something I've discovered about your family — about the famous Swanns. One of your great-aunts, actually. Not sure which — Georgina, I think. I'll find out more details when I go to the Botanic Gardens and the Garden Museum up here. Norwich is where they lived, I understand. Want me to discover more?'

I smiled. 'Of course. Sounds fascinating. What did they get up to? Yes, find out all you can, please, Ben.'

'OK,' he said. 'Must go now — but what are you up to this morning?'

I told him about the school garden, how it was taking shape and sunflower seeds were already planted. How we had some characters among the children. How the whole project was fun. I heard his quiet laugh — like music, sweet and warm — and then I added, without thinking too much, 'When are you coming back, Ben?'

'In a day or two. Don't work too hard — I'll give you a hand when I return. Cheerio for now.' And he was gone.

I spent the afternoon moving summer annual seedlings from the tunnel to the borders, ready for selling and cutting later in the season. The cold spring wind had gone, the sun was warming up, and they would do well.

It was hard work, on my knees, bending and stretching, but by the time I had finished, I felt I'd done a good job. Despite my aching back and earth-encrusted fingernails, how satisfying it was to work with nature. As I put away the tools, watered my small seedlings, and then made my way back to the cottage, I thought of using some of these beauties I'd just planted — daisies, lupins, delphiniums and dahlias — as cut flowers. And why not put some of the arrangements around the nursery for visitors to enjoy when they came to buy their own plants?

If I did as Mrs Bond had suggested, letting people see what I could create, was it possible that my flower career, which at the moment was taking a rest, might start up again here in the village? After supper, I settled down with my laptop, looking for news of fresh interest in the flower world. And when bedtime came, Ben's voice rang in my head. *What could he have discovered about my Great-Aunt Georgina?* I wondered drowsily, and then fell asleep.

★ ★ ★

Ned was opening the post when I got to the office next morning. 'Morning, Miss Rachel,' he said, 'nothing but bills by the look of it . . . No, there *is* one for you — here — ' He tossed it across the desk.

'Thanks,' I said, wondering who had sent me a colourful picture postcard. Someone on holiday, I guessed. But it wasn't a holiday scene — it was an image of a large plant filling the card, with its handsome round flowers, brightest blue with white and gold centres, spilling out and bringing a splash of beauty to the untidy desk.

Uncertain as to what the plant was, or who the card was from, I turned it over.

What do you think of this Mexican beauty? asked Ben's scrawly writing. *Read the details, and I think you'll picture it growing against that rough old wall where my plants are to go. See you soon. Ben.*

I sat back, had another look at the picture — and, yes, I imagined it along that wall, and then read the small print which told me this was Morning Glory, *Ipomoea tricolor*, a Mexican species cultivated in many countries for its showy flowers.

Well! I sat back and looked at Ned who was watching me with a grin all over his face. 'Ben is bringing us one of these,' I told him, and gave him the card to inspect. For a moment he said nothing, then he returned the card to me. 'Mr Dexter sure about this, is he?'

I nodded, solemnly. 'I'm afraid so, Ned.' We looked at each other for a couple of seconds, and then both laughed.

'So be it, Miss Rachel,' he said, getting up and reaching for his hat and thick gloves. 'Mr Dexter wants a jungle out there, and he'll have one. I'll get on with the lettuce seedlings, and there's a customer just come in, if you wouldn't mind seeing to her . . . ' He disappeared out into the nursery, and I went to find the woman.

She was a small, middle-aged lady, carrying a clipboard and looking very authoritative. Rather small eyes looked at me with great determination. 'Are you Rachel Swann?'

'Yes,' I said, and smiled. 'Can I help you?'

'Flowers,' she said, and nodded. 'You're a flower arranger, I believe?'

'Yes. But I work in London . . . '

'I understand you also do very good

arrangements down here in Devon, from this nursery?'

'Well, I have done, but I don't — ' I stopped. What was all this about? And then I recalled my magazine article — was it published already? Things became a little clearer. I widened my smile. 'Please tell me what I can do for you.'

'I am Tessa Browning, Mrs Haworth Jones' secretary. She has asked me to come and see if you would be willing to arrange some flowers for a dinner she is giving quite soon. It's a charity do. She suggests some small vases that could decorate the big kitchen table where the meal will take place. Nothing too elaborate.'

Tessa Browning fixed me with her gaze, and I realized suddenly this was a chance that I must take up. I smiled, and suggested, 'Shall we go and talk it over with a cup of coffee? Come this way, Tessa.' I led her into the little cabin where we sold the plants, and settled her down at a table with a good view outside of a bed of hyacinths, bright blue in the sunshine.

'Coffee? Sugar and milk?' She nodded, saying 'No sugar,' before putting her clipboard on the table in front of her.

As I collected the cups of coffee, found a plate of biscuits, and took the lot into the cabin, my mind was very busy. *Small vases. Cottage garden flowers to decorate a big kitchen.* What fun that would be! And my name might begin to grow, down here in Devon.

We sat together and she thawed a bit, laughing when I told her about the schoolchildren and their new garden, and wondering if Mrs Haworth Jones might not consider a visit to the plot while they were planting their seeds. 'She's fond of children — hers are grown, of course — but I think she would enjoy seeing the local kids learning about nature. I'll suggest it to her. Now — ' And then we were into the world of likely flowers, of vases; and, finally, of costs.

Half an hour later, Tessa left; I felt I had made a new — slightly unlikely — friend, one who would help me to continue my career. I went down the path and found Ned, busy at work with the lettuce seedlings, and told him I was going to grow a lot more cottage flowers because it was likely that I would be asked to make arrangements.

He straightened up, stretched, pulled a face, and then grinned at me. 'Whatever you want, Miss Rachel. We've already got lupins and delphiniums in the tunnel, and they can go out soon. Tell me what else you fancy, and I'll see what I can find . . . ' There was a crowd of customers coming through the front gates, so both he and I went to greet them and see what we could do.

Then it was time for lunch, and after that I knew I must pay a quick visit to Uncle Dexter and see how he had got on at the hospital. Ned looked at me very anxiously. 'We can't go on like this, Miss Rachel — just you and me here, and you needing to see Mr Dexter every day. Wonder if we shouldn't try and find some extra help. What do you think?'

I stood quite still, suddenly understanding what he was saying. My mind churned.

'But Ben will be back in a few days — he can help . . . '

Ned grunted. 'That's not today. Nor perhaps tomorrow. It's now we need the extra hands.' He looked at me with his faded eyes, and I realized how loyal he was to our nursery. He was right, too: we needed help. I wouldn't go and see Uncle Dexter this afternoon. I would go this evening when the nursery was closed.

'All right, Ned,' I said. 'I'll give you a hand with the lettuce, but for the moment we must go and deal with this crowd.' We spent the next hour answering questions, choosing plants, and trying to please our customers. Finally, the lettuces were planted, the nursery closed, and both Ned and I slumped down in our chairs in the office, thankful that the busy day was over.

'Ned, I'll talk to Uncle about some more help. You're quite right, we do need it. Perhaps one of the village ladies might give us a few afternoons . . . '

He sniffed and wiped his forehead

with his bright red handkerchief. 'Got to be someone who knows about gardening,' he said. 'Can't have just anyone . . . 'specially if they don't know a weed from a cabbage!'

I got up and grinned at him. 'All right, you've made your point. Close up now and go home, Ned; after I've had a clean-up, I'm going to see how Uncle Dexter is.'

'Give him my best, Miss Rachel. And tell him we can't wait to have him back again with things as they used to be — that'll be the day!'

I nodded, said *Yes, of course*, but in my mind I was in a different Swann's Nursery, possibly without Uncle Dexter in his office, and with unknown and fresh helpers learning how to deal with the customers. Would I still be here then, or would I have returned to Beautiful Bunches? And where would Ben Hunter be? It was all a tricky problem which I pushed away as I went indoors to clean up and prepare for my visit to Uncle Dexter.

9

The hotel was busy when I arrived, just after six o'clock. The wrong time to call, perhaps, for supper dishes were being taken out of rooms, and the waitressing girls looked very occupied. But I made excuses — *So busy at the nursery during the day!* — and brought Uncle a tiny vase filled with blue hyacinths and a couple of white hellebores, hoping he would enjoy the bright colours.

I saw Mrs Bond whisking downstairs as I went up; she smiled, waved a hand and called back over her shoulder, 'He's finished his meal, do go in,' before disappearing downstairs.

I knocked at his door and his warm voice told me to enter. 'Uncle,' I said, 'sorry, but I couldn't come earlier; so busy this afternoon, lots of customers, so here I am now. How did you get on at the hospital?'

'Dear child, sit you down. So good to see you. Yes, make yourself comfortable.' His smile was broad, and I felt the slight hint of uneasiness, which I had been conscious of all day, fade away.

'Tell me your news,' he went on, and I laughed a bit at that.

'No,' I said, 'it's your news I want! Tell me about your assessment.'

I thought his warm expression tightened a bit, but he still sounded cheerful. 'Went very well. Found nothing wrong with me. I'm all ready for the op next week.'

'So soon? That's splendid.' We looked at each other for a stretching moment, and I guessed he was planning his return to the nursery as soon as possible. I picked my next words very carefully.

'You'll have quite a long convalescence, I expect, Uncle. Have they told you how long it might be before you can start walking again?'

He didn't answer at once, but when he did his voice was firm and his eyes bright. 'No knowing, all depends on how the op goes. But I shall start exercising and get back on my feet pretty soon, I'm sure.'

I nodded, thoughts flying around. 'And what about physiotherapy? Can you go somewhere local for the exercises?'

'Yes, yes, it's all sorted out. Mrs Bond will take me to the clinic in town as many days as I need to go.'

Something was jarring inside me. Mrs Bond seemed to be ready to do everything for him — what could it mean? And how could she run this hotel if she was always driving Uncle around town? I thought hard, and then said quietly, 'She's being so helpful, isn't she? How does she find the time?'

Uncle Dexter sat up straighter, and didn't look at me, but instead stared at the hyacinths I had put on his table. And then, finally, he said sharply: 'She's a remarkable woman, so you don't have to worry about her. Now . . . '

I knew then that Mrs Bond was a subject not to be discussed. We were back to the nursery, so I took a big breath and started talking about being short of hands.

'Ned and I both feel that we need a new member of staff.'

He stared at me. 'You have Ben Hunter — isn't he enough?'

I wriggled in my chair. 'Well, yes, he's a good worker — when he's here. But at the moment, he's away, finding plants to fill in that waste bit of ground which we talked about.'

'Hmmm. The exotics. Yes. But he'll be back in a day or so — well, there's your extra pair of hands. Surely you can manage until then? We don't want any more strangers in the nursery. And anyway, I shall be able to come back before long, even if I can't do any real work — I can man the office, take the calls, do the orders . . .'

Again we looked at each other, and I saw in his eyes the anxiety that I also felt. But I said nothing, just nodded my head and hoped that the operation would go better than I feared. So then I switched subjects: no longer the nursery, but this time my flowers, and the commission to do Mrs Haworth Jones' dinner flowers in a couple of weeks.

'Splendid,' said Uncle Dexter with a gleam in his eyes. 'And will you have enough flowers to fufill the commission? No need to buy in, I hope?'

I smiled. 'We're growing everything I can think of, Uncle, to make these bunches. Just the cottage garden flowers we do so well — and Ned is sowing many more seeds for me. I think I'll manage — I have all sorts of ideas.'

And then we talked about the exotic plants Ben was bringing back. 'One of them is a bright blue flower which will spread all over that old wall — should be a good background for others he might have in mind . . . '

I paused. It seemed now that Ben and his giant plants from other lands had taken root in Uncle Dexter's mind. I wasn't sure whether to be pleased or not. I still preferred the old-fashioned cottage garden flowers — but perhaps the nursery might expand a bit and grow both? Ben had talked of financial expansion, so maybe Uncle agreed with him. And, of course, it was very important that Swann's Nursery continued successfully. I changed the subject, and when I saw Uncle concealing a yawn, I knew it was time to leave him in peace after his challenging day.

'I'll be along again soon,' I said. 'The schoolchildren come again on Friday, and I expect there'll be some funny tales to tell. And, of course, you'll want to talk to Ben about his new plants. Cheerio, Uncle, until then.'

I left him in the peace of his room where, no doubt, he would sit and think until bedtime. I did just wonder, as I left the hotel, whether Mrs Bond would make another visit to him; but that was nothing to do with me.

I was walking along the lane towards the nursery when a car stopped just in front of me, and Teddy Walters opened the door and grinned at me. 'Good timing,' he said. 'Hop in and I'll take you the rest of the way. Or we could just drop in at the pub for a quickie? Got a spare moment, have you, Rache?'

How nice, I thought at once. A friendly chat, a relaxing drink, and then a chance to take the rest of the evening quietly, planning my flower arrangements. So I beamed at him, and got into the car. 'Let's go.'

I expected to spend a happy evening. We chatted, we sipped our drinks, we smiled at each other. But then Teddy said — slowly, and with an expression of what looked like hope on his face — 'What about an evening out, Rache, just you and me, like we used to be? A film? A posh dinner somewhere?'

Suddenly, I tightened up. This wasn't going where I wanted. Yes, he was a friendly, amusing partner for an hour or so . . . but inside me, I recognized a deeper, more urgent need. I wanted to be with someone knowledgeable about flowers; someone who would understand my anxieties about Uncle Dexter, and the future of our family nursery. Teddy's life was bound up in his school and I knew I could never step into that world. For flowers and family meant so much to me.

I saw him watching me, saw his face change from hope to a quick, sharp frown.

'Sorry, Teddy,' I said, 'but — I don't think so. I don't think we're any good together . . . '

'We used to be.' His voice was curt and I nodded, acknowledging the truth of his words.

'I know, but that was quite a long time ago. And since then, we've both gone in different directions.'

He leant closer and put his hand on mine, looking very intently into my eyes. 'There's no reason why we couldn't start again. Come on, Rache, say yes . . . '

But I couldn't. I *wouldn't*, for it wasn't fair to think it might work when I knew it wasn't possible. Teddy and I, a couple? No way.

I smiled at him, slid my hand away from his, and prepared to get up and leave.

And then in that difficult, silent

moment, a new voice came between us, and I knew it was all over.

'I believe you're part of the nursery down the road? Could I talk to you about my herbs?'

I heard Teddy make an exclamation of annoyance, sensed him get up and remove our empty glasses, leaving me looking at the woman standing beside my chair. I rose, switching my thoughts from a possible future with Teddy back to this unexpected moment of having to talk about herbs.

'Yes,' I said, 'I work at the nursery.' I looked at the small basket of greenery she was holding. 'Are these yours? You grew them? They look very healthy — all the popular ones: lavender, mint, sage, chamomile . . . '

The woman smiled, a neat smile that showed good teeth and contented hazel eyes. She said quietly, 'I'm a herbalist, qualified many years ago, and now I grow them for sale. I wonder if you would like to try a few baskets on sale or return?'

We looked at each other, and at once

I found her interesting. She looked at ease, and I thought her to be quite a character, dressed in quietly colourful full skirt and a pale t-shirt covered with herbal motifs. Her silver hair shone in the lamplight, and I found I was glad to smile at her. I wanted to know more.

'We might try a few in the nursery,' I said, 'Mrs — Miss — ?'

'Rosemary Leach. I moved into the village last winter. I'm a widow from upcountry, and I live alone. I want to develop my passion for herbs, and I heard someone say you were in the nursery down the road. So I took the chance — and here I am.'

'I'll be glad to put them on show, Mrs Leach. Could you bring half a dozen baskets tomorrow? We'll discuss sales when you come.'

We exchanged smiles. 'I must go now,' I added, 'so see you tomorrow.'

Teddy was a stiff figure, waiting impatiently by the entrance. In silence, we went into the car park and he drove me home.

'See you on Friday morning, Rache,' he said, with a tight smile, and I nodded.

'All right, Teddy,' I said. 'Sorry about this evening — ' But he merely looked away and drove off without a last smile.

I went into the cottage and told myself this was the end of that small meeting up with Teddy Walters. I climbed the stairs to my bedroom, sadly aware that we had finished our new friendship. But before I slept, I had the sense to remind myself that tomorrow was a new day.

The next morning was brisk, work-wise: deliveries arrived from one of our compost firms, which meant a lot of sacks being lugged about, and we had quite a few customers, keen to get their spring gardens going. And then, out of the blue, a delivery of huge, green-leaved plants, over a metre high, well-packed and being moved very carefully by the two men in the van.

'Where are these from?' I asked as Ned and I tried to determine where they should go.

'Large garden in Norfolk, where it's full of these great big giants. Not the sort of plants I want, thanks very much,' said the driver with a twinkle in his eye.

Of course. Ben's exotics had arrived. I grinned at the man. 'You and me both,' I said, 'but they've got to go somewhere. And I think the best place is down here.'

Together, we went towards the waste patch. 'I'll leave them for you to dig in, shall I?' he asked, once they were leaning against the wall. 'Got another load to deliver this morning, so can't hang about.'

I watched the van drive away, saw Ned frown, and we both decided Ben's plants would have to wait for the collector himself to see to. I got coffee from Katie and we sat in the office, hoping customers would leave us in peace for five minutes. We were chatting about Uncle Dexter's soon-to-come operation, when a familiar voice called out in the nursery: 'Rachel — where are you?'

I got up, discovered I was smiling,

and hurried outside. 'Ben! You're back!'

He stood just outside the office, looking down at the tunnel and the glasshouse, and I thought the expression on his face was a happy one. I wondered if he was as glad to be back as I was to see him, and if I should be pleased if he was; and I knew, suddenly, that Ben had become an essential part of Swann's Nursery.

I went up to him. 'Welcome back, Ben.' He said, 'Thanks,' and we looked at each other for what seemed a ridiculously long moment. Until Ned came out of the office and, passing Ben on his way to the tunnel to see to his seedlings, commented: 'All your giant plants are waiting for you by the wall down there, Mr Hunter. Better get on and put them in, hadn't you? No point in hanging around . . . '

Ben and I grinned at each other, and quickly started walking down to the old waste patch, talking all the while as we went.

10

'How's your uncle?' he asked as we reached the waste ground and he saw all the plants piled up there against the wall. And even as I told him about the operation next week, he fell silent, going up to the giant specimens and fingering their enormous leaves. I watched his expression. He was looking at these monsters as if they needed all the tender loving care he could find to give them. And then he turned to me.

'Look, Rachel, I'll just go and change into my work clothes, and then I must get on with planting these. I'm afraid they'll keep me busy for an hour or so, but after that I'll be able to help you. Can you manage on your own with Ned for this afternoon?'

I nodded. 'Of course. Perhaps I can help later on?'

He paused, heading for the cottage,

and looked back at me. 'Fixing up the hose would be great — please?'

'All right. Off you go. I'll keep watch on these babies till you come back!'

I saw Rosemary Leach putting down the last of twelve baskets on the terrace in front of the office, and I hurried back to her. 'So you've come with your baskets of herbs — how fresh they look. Let's put them over here at the side of this display stand.'

We arranged them tidily at the foot of the stand of the pretty little alpines, and then I looked at her. 'What sort of price are you asking, Mrs Leach? We can't pay much, I'm afraid.'

She named a price which I thought was reasonable. They were, after all, home-grown, very fresh, and set in those attractive little baskets. I could see them selling quite well; and indeed, almost at once, a customer came up and looked at them, asking what sort of herbs they were.

I left Rosemary to reply, seeing how she smiled and seemed glad to talk about her plants. 'This is tarragon,' she said, fingering a tall green stem. 'Lovely with chicken, and perhaps fish. And then you've got mint to go with new potatoes, and some sage for your sausages, and of course parsley for a garnish. Everything you need in the kitchen!'

I stood back, listening and watching, and it struck me that here was someone who — like my uncle and Ben, like Ned and me — loved her plants. Someone who it might be helpful to have here in the nursery. But I kept the thought to myself, and decided I would talk to Uncle Dexter about Rosemary Leach and her herbs when I next visited him. I smiled at her as she said goodbye, and suggested she should call in in another few days, to see how her herbs had sold.

Her smile was very warm. 'Thank you,' she said. 'I shall look forward to seeing you again — and I understand you are the niece of the owner of this lovely little nursery? It really is beautiful.' She looked over the flower beds with such a longing expression on her face that I smiled and said, 'Please have a wander around, if you would like to. There's plenty to see.'

'Thank you, yes, I would love to.' I watched her at once head off down the path beside the summer border, where very soon all the wonderful old cottage garden flowers would be blooming.

Then I remembered Ben's exotics, and went to undo the hose and get it all ready for his planting. And as I undid the coils and arranged them neatly along the paths leading to the waste ground, my head was full of thoughts of flowers and how beautiful they were, and how most people loved them. It struck me, as I worked, that until now, my interest in flowers had been based purely on what I could do with them, how I could arrange them into eye-catching groups which people would pay a lot of money for: arrangements and installations. But now, suddenly, I was changing my ideas; flowers were living things which, with hard work and knowledge and a lot of tender loving care, grew into the most beautiful gardens which enhanced everybody's lives . . .

I remained in that lovely flower world, drifting into memories of gardens that Uncle Dexter had taken me around as I grew up. The pictures in my mind grew into fields of grass and wildflowers, full of butterflies, bees and grasshoppers; then into woodlands full of sweet-scented bluebells, where we had holiday picnics. The wonderful countryside, in all its natural splendour.

And by the time I had spread out the hose and connected it to the water source, I had allowed my thoughts to go on into a different, stranger world. I was thinking then of Great-Aunt Georgina, who must have shared my love of nature — indeed, I supposed that to become a plant collector, and particularly for an Edwardian lady, that love must have grown into an obsession.

So when Ben arrived at my side, I was still in that dream world, staring at his new plants, until —

'Rachel, thanks for fixing up the hose.' His quiet voice jerked me back to reality.

I swung around and met his eyes, looking at me with amusement, and a certain curiosity.

'Ben, please tell me what you found out about Georgina Swann — I can't wait to know!'

The amusement slid into a slight frown. 'I'll tell you later, after we've done this job.' He began to unfold his plants, and make tidy spaces for them. But I was at his side, hands doing what I could to help with the planting, although my mind was still full of the portrait of the tall woman in her high-necked dress and shady hat.

'No,' I said. 'I need to know now — come on Ben, tell me what you found out!'

Again he paused in his work, looking at me with a grin. 'Impatient creature, aren't you? All right, just hang on while I put this ipomoea into the ground and water it. This is the blue morning glory that will cover the wall — can you imagine it?'

And I could. Brilliant, blue and white scented flowers making a beautiful background to the huge, dark-leaved giants he was now putting into the ground, composting and watering with such expertise and satisfaction. He worked on, and slowly told me about visiting the Botanical Gardens and Garden Museum in Norfolk, near the big house where the Swann family lived, before Grandfather Swann came into Devon and started his nursery in this village. I listened, enthralled.

'Your great-aunts were very different, apparently. Sophie was shy and biddable, preferred painting to gardening, married the man her father approved of, and had a well-behaved family. Your Uncle Dexter is part of that branch, it appears.'

He straightened his back, wiped his forehead and looked at me with a big grin. 'But your Great-Aunt Georgina — oh, no, quite the opposite. Off on her travels despite her father's disapproval, searching for unknown handsome plants to bring back to this country, for all the rich owners of big houses who wanted new gardens with which to build their fame. Your aunt did that — and also painted the plants she saw. She has an exhibition up at Kew Gardens — something you should visit, perhaps.'

The last plant was in, and now the waste ground — free of weeds, well-dug-over, fed and watered — was the home of Swann Nursery's latest acquisitions. I stood there, looking at these foreigners, certainly very handsome and unusual, and wondered how Great-Aunt Georgina would have felt, had she known about them growing here in the family nursery.

I realized Ben had stopped working, was gathering his tools, and now standing there, watching me. I wondered what he would think if he knew what was in my mind — but instead of going on about Great-Aunt Georgina, he touched my arm and said — quietly, and with that warm smile that I enjoyed so much when it appeared — 'Wake up, Rachel! Time to go in and clean up, I think.

And then I've got an idea — how about a little outing this evening, wandering around this beautiful countryside with a picnic in our pockets?'

That really brought me back to the present. A picnic! Of course I'd love it. I jumped at the idea as I helped him roll up the hose again. 'Ben, that would be wonderful — shall we ask Katie to pack us up some sandwiches?'

He pushed the hose along the path, back towards the tunnel where it lived, and said over his shoulder, 'I've got a better idea than that. While you go and change, I'll walk up to the chippie in the village and get us a good package of fish and chips — would that suit you?'

I laughed. 'It certainly would. And shall we take a drink with us?'

He paused at the entrance to the tunnel, looking back at me. 'What's wrong with river water? I've drunk enough of it to know it's safe — and fresh and beautiful. OK by you?'

'Yes!' I watched him cleaning and then putting away the spade and the trowels, saw him talking to Ned who was just about to lock up the office and go home, when suddenly I remembered that Rosemary Leach was still in the nursery — where? I looked all around, and then saw her, coming towards me, her face alive with pleasure.

'What beautiful plants you grow here,' she said. 'I have so enjoyed looking at them all — and I do hope my herbs will sell for you. Please let me know if you need any more, won't you?'

I walked with her to the entrance, where we paused and smiled at each other. It was in my mind to suggest she might like to come to the nursery and do some light work a few days a week, but then I thought I must consult with Uncle Dexter first. So I said yes, and watched her set off up the road, no doubt heading for her home. And then I went into the cottage to clean up and prepare for Ben's lovely outing.

Yes, we would go into the fields that bordered the river: there would be late sunlight shafting through the trees, birds, and possibly a heron fishing in the shallows. After I pulled off my trousers and put on a cotton skirt for a change, I brushed my hair, looked in the mirror, and thought that the Rachel Swann who looked back at me had something new about her. And then I went down to find Ben.

He was waiting for me, shabby back-pack on his back, in clean trousers and a fresh shirt. His smile was welcoming and he patted the pack. 'All here, keeping warm for us until we find a good picnic place. Are you ready for a stroll, Rachel?'

I felt my smile glow. 'I certainly am! I know a lovely spot down by the river — there's a path we can take which was my secret place as a child . . . This way, Ben.'

How delightful that stroll was. The sun was warm, already painting the sky with its myriad setting palette, and a welcome breeze touched us as we walked down through the field. We talked — how we talked. About the new plants. About

Uncle Dexter, whom we must visit tomorrow morning. About Rosemary Leach's herbs — Ben was interested, and thought they would sell well. And, of course, about Great-Aunt Georgina, and her artwork up in Kew Gardens.

'There's a pavilion of paintings by collectors,' Ben told me, 'and one panel of them shows your aunt's work. You really should visit, Rachel.' He turned, gave me a keen look. 'After all, she's famous — and once you see her paintings you'll respect her even more. Imagine being her, wearing corsets and long skirts, yet putting up with all the dangers and difficulties of cleaving her way through jungles of enormous plants.'

I led him down to the river, grey-green and peaceful this evening, swirling along with its own soft music. Such a magical place, with its wildlife all around us, and the quiet serenity of early evening.

He took my hand and led me to a handy rock where we could sit. 'Will you be comfy enough, Rachel?' I nodded as I found a perch among the moss and lichen covering it.

'I'm fine. And you?'

He nodded. 'A feather bed after some of the picnic spots I had to find abroad.'

We smiled at each other, and I felt a new feeling spread through me: a sort of happiness that was different and very important, promising me another exciting dimension to my life. Flowers, yes; family . . . and now Ben and our mutual love of the countryside.

Ben unwrapped our supper and we ate slowly, with great enjoyment. When we had finished, he wrapped up the papers, put them in the backpack, and then took out a small plastic cup which he carried down to the river, filled with water, and brought back to me.

'A toast to your career, Rachel — when you get back to it,' he said, smiling and sitting down again.

I sipped the water. Icy, clean and sparkling, it did something to stimulate my emotions; and I said, very quietly, 'Thanks, Ben, but the career doesn't seem quite so important now — when I think of the nursery and all the work needed there; and this amazing country-side which I love so much — and then there's Great-Aunt Georgina to think about, to admire, and to wish I had known her.'

He took the half-empty cup from me, finished the water, and then looked very directly into my eyes. 'You sound as if your ideas are changing, Rachel. Not a bad thing when it happens like this. That's how I knew I wanted to collect plants — new ideas, new ambitions.'

We sat on in silence, our thoughts perhaps mingling. And then a movement in the reeds caught my eye. 'Look,' I said, 'a heron, fishing . . . what would Great-Aunt Georgina have done when she saw that, I wonder?'

Ben paused before saying, slowly, 'She would have probably included it in one of her pictures. I think she was a lady who dealt with whatever life threw at her. She was somebody who knew her own mind.'

11

The evening was drawing in as we made our way back to the nursery grounds, in a comfortable, companionable silence. And then Ben stopped, looking at me with those intense eyes, as he said, very quietly, 'I have something else to tell you about Georgina Swann, Rachel — something more important than the fact that she was a famous plant collector. I think you'll be surprised.'

I looked at him in amazement. What on earth had Great-Aunt Georgina done that could really surprise me now? She had been a wayward daughter who took charge of her life, and went travelling as few other Edwardian women had the courage to do — but what else had Ben discovered?

I grinned at him. 'Go on, then, tell me — this sounds extraordinary.'

For a moment he was silent. 'Be prepared for something really dramatic, Rachel,' he said, and his voice was gentle. He took hold of my hands and looked into my wide eyes.

'Your great-aunt was unmarried, but had a child,' he said very quietly. His hands were warm about mine, strong and comforting; for suddenly I felt disturbed at such unexpected news.

I gulped, and as my thoughts whirled around, said slowly, 'An illegitimate child — in those days — so whatever did her family think?'

He dropped my hands, put an arm around my shoulders and slowly walked me back towards the cottage. 'I imagine they were shocked. Especially her father. For, according to the records in the Garden Museum, she packed up very soon after having the baby, leaving it with a friendly family to bring up, and then started her travelling. And that started her painting career.'

I stared at him, thoughts racing. 'She — abandoned her child?'

'I'm afraid so. But we don't know how she felt, how the family felt. We shouldn't really think too badly of her without knowing, Rachel.' He met my stare with a gentle smile, and I thought, *He has kinder thoughts than me . . .*

'All this that you found out — is there any more? Can anyone discover where this child — she, he? — lived? And what happened to the family once the child had grown up? Can we possibly find out?'

Ben stood at my side, silent for a moment, and I saw his thoughts chasing each other across his face. Then, slowly, he said, 'Well, of course, one can always use the Internet to find out. I mean, I have to confess that when you first showed an interest in Great-Aunt Georgina, I used your office computer to track down the basic facts about her. If you really want me to, I could find some more information — I imagine there will be plenty out there, if we really looked for it.'

The shadows were falling now, and

the nursery had that quiet, peaceful atmosphere about it which was so lovely at night. I turned, left him, and wandered down to the beds where the young delphiniums and lupins were throwing up their first colourful spires. I waited for inspiration to come, and slowly it did. Again, I turned and looked back at Ben, who stood there, very still, watching me. I found a smile. He had been so good, so kind, and now he was offering to help even more. And the strong feeling grew inside me: yes, I did want to know about the forgotten child of the Swann family. I needed to know.

I walked back to him, put my hand on his arm and smiled up into his watchful face. 'Yes, Ben, I want you to do that, if you would — please. But perhaps we should tell Uncle Dexter about this first — and ask his permission. What do you think?'

'Yes, you're right. Let's go and see him tomorrow morning, before things get too busy here. After all, any other relative we might track down would be his distant cousin or something — so he needs to agree.'

We stood there for a stretching moment while the sky darkened and bats flew out from the eaves of the cottage. We smiled at each other and then, very carefully, he bent his head and kissed me. First of all on my cheek — and then, as he understood how I felt, he put his lips on mine and waited to see if I would respond. I did. A wonderful kiss: warm, strong, exciting.

I came up for breath and smiled into his calm eyes as he said, 'Rachel, don't let this worry you. I feel that your great-aunt knew what she was doing, and that the child's loss didn't hurt her too much. Obviously her career was more important to her. And perhaps, if we can find out a bit more, it will be helpful for today's family to find a new relative?'

I lay back against his chest, smiling and filled with new, different thoughts. 'Yes, Ben. I agree. Yes, tomorrow we must go and see Uncle Dexter and tell him.'

'And now you should go in and get your beauty sleep. Not that you need it . . . ' And he turned me towards the cottage, nodded as I headed for the door.

'Goodnight, Ben — and thanks for a lovely evening.'

I closed the door behind me and went up to my bed. Truly a magical evening, and the promise of a future full of new possibilities.

★   ★   ★

We found Uncle Dexter in his chair, with a frown on his face. 'Ah, thank goodness for a couple of friendly smiles,' he greeted us, and then his own smile appeared. 'Sorry, but there's been a bit of a spat here. Mrs Bond, you see . . . '

I kissed him, and Ben held out his hand. 'Come to report on the new plants, sir.'

'Yes,' said Uncle, suddenly interested

and with new strength in his voice. 'Planted, are they? Looking good? And what have you brought us?'

I pulled up chairs and we sat down, Ben beside Uncle. He took some paper from his pocket. 'All here, Latin names and all — I'm sure you'll know them — and I think the new bed will look quite dramatic once they've started growing. The blue flowers along the wall, some purple bell flowers lower down, and a bird of paradise pushing its amazing blooms up in the middle . . . that should make an impact, all right, with its brilliant colours and shapes. Oh, and if you agree, I'm thinking of adding an orchid. There's a handy tree branch next the bed where it could attach itself.'

Uncle Dexter didn't answer for a moment, but looked across at me, and I could see him wondering what I might be about to say — to argue, perhaps? To say something detrimental to the new relationship growing between myself and this new young manager of his nursery? But I was learning fast. I said nothing, met his eyes, smiled and nodded.

He smiled back. 'It all sounds very exciting, Ben. I can't wait to get back home and see for myself. Well, the op is very soon, so perhaps shortly afterwards I shall be there.'

I caught a quick glance from Ben, understood that his thoughts echoed mine, and allowed my eyes to accept what was going through his mind. But it was necessary to cheer Uncle along, so I just said, 'Of course, and we shall all be thinking of you and waiting for results. Will — er — Mrs Bond take you to the hospital, Uncle, or can I?'

Another short pause. 'Mrs Bond is being rather authoritative about taking me here and there, Rachel,' Uncle said in a clipped, short voice. 'And so, for the moment, to avoid any unpleasantness, I am accepting her offers. Just so long as you — and Ben — and perhaps Ned and Katie — come to see me after the operation. I shall need all the support I can get, I expect.' But he was smiling again, and so I got up, kissed him, and decided quickly that this was no time to tell him about possible relatives somewhere, for clearly he had enough on his mind.

A few minutes later, as we walked quickly down the lane, returning to the nursery, I said to Ben, 'We couldn't possibly tell him about Great-Aunt Georgina just now, could we?'

'No,' said Ben, 'of course not.' And then we fell silent, but our thoughts were still with Uncle, and the difficult and unwanted relationship which seemed to be arising between him and Mrs Bond.

Later that afternoon, I had a phone call from Tessa Browning. 'Calling to remind you about the flower commission you are doing for Mrs Haworth Jones's supper party, Rachel. Just a few details . . . '

'Yes,' I said, my mind at once busily going around the garden, wondering which flowers I would choose for the small vases she wanted. 'Any ideas about colour, Tessa? What date is the party? And can I arrive early to set up my arrangements?'

I heard papers being rattled, and then she said, 'It's on Friday the 24th — that's the end of this week. The meal will be served at eight o'clock, so come early to do your flowers, and I'll be there to help with vases and water and so on. As for colours — well, the kitchen is plain white, so really anything you choose will provide a lovely spot of colour. We're all looking forward to seeing your flowers. And one last thing. Mrs Haworth Jones particularly wants you to bring a partner. I mean . . . ' She stopped, and I sensed her embarrassment. Did I have a partner? Who knew? And then she added, 'Or at least a friend. Mrs HJ likes to meet new people, you see.'

I swallowed my amusement. 'Thank you, Tessa, that will be very nice. I shall arrive before seven o'clock and bring the vases and flowers with me, and of course I shall be grateful for your help. See you then — goodbye.'

I went down the garden towards the

raised vegetable beds where Ned was planting out the young new plants of salad growth, and helped him with the remainder of his large box of seedlings. We chatted a bit about Uncle Dexter and his hope to see all his friendly staff after the op.

'O'course,' said Ned, nodding his head. 'I'll be there — and Katie, I bet. And then we've just gotta wait and see how it goes, eh?'

'Yes, Ned. We mustn't hope for too much, but even so — I *am* hoping.'

'Me too.'

We finished planting out, and then I returned to the office to look at some new seeds which had just arrived. As I went, I passed Ben, dealing with an elderly man who was looking at the exotics bed by the wall. I overhead his comments, and smiled to myself.

'Well, something new, aren't they? And I like those tall shiny leaves — when they start blooming, and if you can give me enough information to know how to grow them, I might well order a few.

Make a big difference to my ordinary little garden . . . ' Laughter, in which Ben joined, and I caught his eye as he accompanied his customer to the entrance.

And at once I thought, *I'll ask Ben to come with me to the Manor. I'd like him to be beside me. Wonder if he'll say yes? Oh, and what about a haircut and a new shirt?* As if that mattered! And then I was laughing, so loud and so long that Ned looked at me with a frown, shaking his head as he went to sit behind his desk and sort out the seed packets I was looking at.

'You sound happy, Miss Rachel,' he grunted, and as I left the office and went towards the cottage for a welcome cup of tea, I thought, *I am. Goodness, I am happy . . .*

That evening, when Ben disappeared into the office, saying he would do some work on the computer, I wandered around the nursery, making a list in my mind of the flowers that would fill Mrs Haworth Jones's kitchen on Friday. It was still only early April, so I didn't have too much to choose from. The daffodils were all over, only the white narcissus slowly showing buds; they would be a start, and with them I would put some green leaves from the fast-growing willow tree, and perhaps a few of the hellebores still in bloom — pink and white, how lovely they were. Next, some purple honesty half-moons; and then, just to make the colours explode, a few lime-green big, flat flowers of the wild alexanders growing in nearby hedges. I would pick them soon. As I passed the remaining baskets of herbs, I decided to add a final sprig of blue rosemary, and then thought, *Yes, all of them from the nursery, they will really make a show in a plain white kitchen. And now for the vases . . .*

I went into the office and looked around the shelves. Uncle collected odd little containers, and there were one or two there that I could use. A pale blue poison bottle from Victorian times, which would hold a couple of blooms;

an old marmalade galley pot of stoneware, just the job for the herbs and the wild flowers; and an ancient bit of honey-coloured pottery which looked like a much-used cream jar. With those in mind, I went into the cottage and looked along Katie's shelves and in her cupboards, until I had found half a dozen containers which seemed the right sizes and colours, and with a sort of atmosphere about them which made me want to fill them with my flowers at once. But I had to wait until the day before the party for picking — which would be Friday.

Then I remembered: Uncle's operation was fixed for Thursday. And everything else went out of my mind.

12

Ben said he would love to come to the supper. He looked at me a bit strangely, adding, 'I thought you'd probably ask your friend the headmaster. Oh, well.' And then, 'Do I need a haircut?'

'Of course not. You just look — well, rather creative, but make sure you comb it down tidily.' And then I covered my mouth, embarrassed. 'Sorry, Ben. I love your hair. I didn't mean to make personal remarks . . . '

He grinned, shook his head. 'I can take anything you say, Rachel. You know what you're doing, you see.'

Did I? Well, that was a compliment and a half, even if I couldn't quite believe it. I didn't say any more, but gave him my warmest smile, thinking how our relationship seemed to be getting better and better. Nowadays I thought of things to ask him, tell him, surprise him with

— such as, 'School garden on Friday, Ben, and we must watch what young Gareth is doing with his runner beans. Keep an eye on him, because I think he'll want to take over the nursery before he's much older . . . '

Ben stopped what he was doing and turned to look at me. 'Changing the subject to help in the garden, I wondered if Mrs Leach might offer an hour or two — what do you think, Rachel? We could do with the assistance, you know, now that customers are getting excited about their own plots. Could you agree to that? I thought I'd call on her this evening, if you do.'

I thought for a moment. We should really ask Uncle Dexter . . . but not now, with his op so close. I nodded. 'Yes, it's a good idea. And I'd like to come with you when you go — after supper, d'you think?'

He gave me that big smile before turning away again. 'Right, something to look forward to — be ready when you are.'

I got on with my chores, but knew that something was thawing inside me. Ben and I seemed to work together rather well these days. I had pleasant thoughts of going to the Manor supper party with him: he would probably tell our hostess about his adventures searching for exotic plants. I looked forward to hearing his tales, because they interested me. Suddenly, it struck — just like my Great-Aunt Georgina, he longed to find new plants.

Great-Aunt Georgina again . . . I was back with the thought of the abandoned baby. Where might he — or she — have ended up? With a happy life, a marriage — a family, even? Would we ever know? I guessed Ben would soon be making time to use the office computer to find out.

After supper we walked down the lane towards Rosemary Leach's home at the far end of the village, hoping to find her in. Yes, she was in the garden, bending over a very green- and rich-looking bed of tall herbs. Seeing us, she straightened up, invited us in, and suggested we sit on her small terrace where chairs and a table were set out.

'I can offer herb tea, or perhaps a glass of something a little stronger . . . ' Her smile was welcoming, and although I settled for a mint tea, Ben accepted the other offer.

Soon we were all three sitting there, with the scent of roses and herbs wafting about in the evening air. Ben looked at me, and I nodded. Clearly, it was my place to make the offer of employment.

I said, 'Rosemary, your herbs are selling very well, but that's not why we are here. As you are clearly so knowledgeable about growing plants, we wondered if you might be able to give us a few hours of work at the nursery? Customers are coming in now, and it's all hands to the pumps with my uncle away . . . '

She was quiet for a moment, then said, 'Your uncle is the owner of Swann's Nursery, isn't he? I think someone in the village told me that. An unusual name — somehow it rings a vague bell in my mind . . . but there, I'm getting old, can't remember things so clearly now!' She laughed, and we smiled in return. Then she said, 'I should very much enjoy working in the nursery, Rachel. Perhaps a few hours a week — would that be helpful?'

I looked at Ben, and he nodded. 'It would indeed, Rosemary, and we would enjoy having you with us. When can you start?'

'I can manage Tuesday mornings and Wednesday afternoons, and perhaps Friday mornings. Would that be any good?'

Ben looked at me, and I knew it was my turn. 'That would be great, Rosemary. Let's make an arrangement for next week, then. Tuesday morning, eight-thirty until lunchtime?'

Rosemary's pale face flushed slightly and I thought happiness shone in her hazel eyes. A warm feeling spread through me, and although I wondered slightly what Uncle Dexter might say, I knew we had done the right thing: a new member of staff, someone who loved plants as we all did. Nothing could be wrong with that.

After a bit more chat, Ben and I got up and left. I knew he wanted to get to the computer, and I had some emails to answer. But it had been a very pleasant interlude, and as we walked back together, I had a strange feeling that my life was changing — and all for the better.

Later that evening, up in my room with my laptop, I found an email from the flower-arranging magazine, inviting me to take part in a competition they were running. *Yes*, I thought, *why not?* With Rosemary now coming in to help, I felt I could easily do an arrangement and photograph it, then email it through to the competition.

The theme was *Handsome and Out of the Ordinary*. Goodness, that made me think a bit! Going to bed, I let my mind wander around the nursery looking for plants to fill the category, and found it slightly difficult. Until it came to me — what about one of Ben's strange flowers? Certainly handsome — and definitely out of the ordinary! I went to sleep with my mind running around in circles, and dreamed of unknown blossoms.

At breakfast, Ben leaned across the table and said quietly, 'I found out a bit about the baby, Rachel. And you'll be glad to know he survived.'

I dropped my piece of toast in surprise. 'He? Oh, that's wonderful! And what was he called?'

Ben drank his coffee before replying, and I saw the interest on his face. 'Samuel Swann. And now I've got to find out what he did and where he landed up. This evening, perhaps I'll have another go. Can't stop now, those plants need looking at. See you later.'

He left the cottage, and I slowly finished my toast and cup of coffee, thinking all the while about this new and previously unknown member of my family. I felt excited, and full of wonder — where would all Ben's searching eventually take us?

But then Ned came knocking on the door. 'Customers wanting information, Miss Rachel. Can you come?'

I went into the nursery, switching my thoughts from distant relatives living years ago to advice about growing plants in the shade as opposed to full sun. And so the day rushed past.

I found Ben rather silent at supper-time, keen to disappear into the office and sit at the computer. He nodded at me as he left the cottage, and I was disappointed — I had been ready to tell him about the competition, and per-haps ask if I might use one of his amazing flowers.

But that would have to wait. Instead, I walked up the road and paid a visit to my uncle.

He was sitting in his chair, nursing a half-empty glass of something which I imagined kind Mrs Bond had acquired for him. I kissed him, drew my chair up beside him, and asked how he was doing.

He paused before replying, and I saw anxiety spreading over his face. 'Well, Rachel, I'm worrying about quite a few things. Like, will the operation next week do the job on my legs? Will I come back to the nursery? And if not . . . ' Another pause, and I took his hand in mine.

No good saying *Of course it will all work out*, when both he and I — and Ned and Katie and Ben — knew it might not. I said nothing, but waited for his customary sensibility to return.

Then he looked at me, smiled while he shook his head, and said slowly, 'For, you see, I can't stay here. Even though Mrs Bond thinks I can — and ought to. In fact — ' And now he chuckled, and I smiled, too. ' — in fact, she has made an offer which is hard to refuse.'

Goodness, I thought, *surely not marriage?* I said warily, 'Well, she's been very good to you so far — what's her future plan, then, Uncle?'

He moved his legs painfully, and looked at the now empty glass, and then back at me. A sort of grin appeared. 'She wants me to help her run this hotel — a partnership, with me doing the business while she looks after the guests. Hmm. Well, I don't know . . . '

But I knew. It would never work: not between authoritative Mrs Bond and my practical, sensitive uncle — who, even if his legs no longer worked, had a brain and needs she could never fulfil.

I grinned back at him, trying to resolve the situation. 'Forget that kind offer, Uncle,' I said lightly. 'If it's necessary, we'll have you back in the cottage with your wheelchair, waiting for the morning inspection of the nursery. And I think Katie would be delighted to have you back home, so don't worry any more. Let's just wait and see what happens. And now I must tell you about our new helper, Rosemary Leach . . . '

At once, the worry lines faded and new interest shone in his eyes. 'A helper? Tell me all, dear child, I can't wait . . . '

'Well,' I said, 'she appeared out of the blue — with her baskets of herbs, which have been selling very fast: so well-grown, and such good plants. And then she had a look around the nursery and admired it, and then Ben and I thought . . . well, we asked her, and she is going to come and help out three times a week. Uncle, I do hope you agree . . . it was because Ned said we needed someone else to work with us.'

I looked at him, a little anxiously, but he was nodding, and his eyes had that shine that meant he was happier with life. 'If old Ned thinks we need help, then we do. So yes, child, it sounds as if you and young Ben have made a good decision.' He stopped, thought, and then commented, 'I'd like to meet this good lady — what's her name, Rosemary? Like one of her herbs, eh?' He was chuckling.

How relieved I was. Uncle's word had always been law before, but now it seemed he was trying to work *with* us. I said happily, 'I'll ask Rosemary to come here with me the next time she's at the nursery — on her way home, perhaps.'

'Good idea. But don't forget — Thursday is the big day.'

My smile faded. 'I can't possibly forget, Uncle. And I'll be in the hospital the very next day to see how you are.'

'Yes. I shall be glad to see you. And to know just what my future holds.'

We were quiet for a moment, both of us thinking of what might lie ahead. But then he was smiling again. 'And what about your flower arrangements? Are you doing any? Not much time for that at the moment, I suppose.'

So I told him about the competition, and he laughed. 'Handsome? And out of the ordinary? Not much the nursery can help you with there, then. I don't think cottage garden flowers, bless their hearts, could be called 'Out of the Ordinary', do you?'

'No,' I said, 'not really. But perhaps some wildflowers mixed with a few not-so-common ones, and then a really spectacular flower to top it all off. I'm thinking about it, Uncle, and I'll let you see the photo when it's done.'

A knock at the door, and Mrs Bond poked her head inside, smiling at me and carrying the evening newspaper. 'Thought you would like to see this, Mr Swann.'

I got up. Yes, time to leave them to sort out whatever relationship was going on there. I kissed Uncle, smiled politely at Mrs Bond — who was clearly waiting to be invited to sit down — and left them to it.

My head full of thoughts, I walked back to the nursery and found Ben wandering among the flower beds. He looked up as I approached. 'Ah, there you are — I wondered where you'd got to. Rachel, I have some more news about your Great-Aunt Georgina and her abandoned son, Samuel. Shall we go in and sit down, and I'll tell you — it's quite exciting, actually.'

A little throb of excitement started

inside me. 'Yes, of course — indoors?'

'How about an evening nightcap of coffee and family revelations?' He grinned, took my arm, and we walked quickly towards the cottage.

13

With the coffee pot on the table and a plate of Katie's shortbread between us, I sat impatiently, staring at Ben and willing him to tell me what he had discovered. He was silent for too long a while, so I urged him on. 'Go on, for goodness sake, tell me!'

He grinned at me, took a notebook from his pocket and flipped the pages. 'What an impatient creature you are — but here he is . . . '

He read from the pages. 'Samuel Swann, married a lady called Alice in the village where he was born, and slowly got involved in her family's farm. So much so that when her old father died, he took it over and began running it — successfully, it seems. But remember, life was hard on the land in those days, and I don't suppose they made much money. And they had two children — a boy, Thomas; and a girl, Winifred. And it's Winnie that we're interested in.' He took a bite of shortbread and I knew I had to be patient.

'Yes,' I said, trying to keep the words quiet and slow. 'So what did Winnie get up to?'

He looked at the notebook again. 'She grew up and married someone called Joseph Manning, and they had a child: a daughter called Elfrida.' He grinned at me. 'Names were a bit fancy in those days, you see. But the fascinating thing is what Elfrida did with her life.'

Excitement grew, but somehow I controlled myself. 'Please tell me.'

'All right. She founded a large family: daughters and sons — and a late daughter by the name of Pauline, who married — ' He looked at me, and his eyes twinkled. ' — a chap called Leach.'

I gasped. 'I don't believe it! You mean that Rosemary, our Rosemary, comes from the Swann family, but a different branch of it? Wow! That's terrific!'

We sat back, suddenly silent, although my thoughts were rushing about like mad things. Of course, families quickly changed names when children got married, so relationships changed, too. But this was amazing!

Slowly, my mind sorted itself out. I looked at Ben and asked, 'So what this means is that Uncle Dexter is distantly related to Rosemary Leach of the herbs?'

'Seems like it. Needs a bit more sorting out; but yes, I would say he is a very distant cousin of some degree.'

I sank into another silence, thinking. 'Should we tell Uncle Dexter, do you think? I mean — now, just before his op?'

Ben pondered. 'I think we should wait until it's over. He will have the chance to relax while he's recuperating, to think about new things, so then we could tell him. If you agree. After all, Rachel, this is your family, not mine.'

'But you're doing all the work — oh, Ben, I'm so grateful. And now, when I look at that picture of Great-Aunt Georgina in her finery, I shall realize that she was not just a famous plant collector and painter, but an ancestor worth having because of all the cousins she has given us!'

Ben smiled, folded the notebook and put it back in his pocket. 'Bedtime, I think. We've a busy day tomorrow. You've got flowers to pick, haven't you, for Friday night? I must find a decent shirt, and the gardening schoolkids will be here on Friday morning — let's save our energy, shall we?'

He laughed, and I joined in. 'We lead such an exciting life!'

★ ★ ★

The days swept past. On Wednesday morning, I crept away because Rosemary could take my place, with Ned's help, and I took the bus into town. The big department store was a jewel box of pretty dresses, and I chose a slimline silky one in a beautiful fuschia colour. I looked — well, I thought I did — quite elegant in it. And then on the way out, passing the men's counter, I saw a very nice shirt, white with a tiny greeny-blue check on it, and I thought at once of Ben's eyes. This would be a wonderful match — why didn't I buy it for him? A present in return for all the work he was doing, both for the nursery and for my family. I hurried home, pleased with myself and my purchases.

And then I started to worry. Was it tactless of me to give Ben a decent shirt? Because I wanted us both to look nice at the supper party on Friday night? What would he think? Say? *Oh, dear* . . . I knew then that I had done a silly thing. I returned to work, telling myself firmly that if Ben didn't want the shirt, Uncle Dexter would love to have it. It wouldn't be wasted.

Later that afternoon, Ben found me in the wild part of the garden, where the untidy hedge was beginning to sway and swing in the breeze as the tall cow parsley stems grew and grew. I was thinking that cow parsley, arranged with something rather dramatic, might well fulfil the theme of the competition of Out of the Ordinary . . .

His voice brought me back to everyday things. 'So, where did you disappear to? I wanted to talk to you about whether we should tell Rosemary Leach what I've found out — what do you think, Rachel?'

I looked at him for a long moment. The sun had already touched his handsome face, and browning skin wrinkled around those lustrous greeny-blue eyes. Such a handsome man . . . but my mind added something very important: a man who behaved handsomely, too, with good manners and great kindness. And suddenly I understood that Ben Hunter was having a very good effect on me. When I came back to the nursery I had been uptight with resentment at having to leave my excellent and fascinating job at Beautiful Bunches. And now I felt very different. Happy to be here. Calming down a bit. Glad to be of help to Uncle, and ready to do whatever I could should his operation not be as successful as he was hoping.

So I smiled warmly at Ben and said

quietly, 'I'll do whatever you think best, Ben. I don't want it to be too much of a shock, though. Perhaps we should hint that we would like to talk to her one evening . . . is that a good idea?'

He nodded, looked at the hedge where the lovely cow parsley was dancing in the breeze, and then said, 'Why don't we wait for a bit? Until Friday evening is over, and my plans are properly laid.'

My stomach turned over. My smile died. I stared at him, and my voice sounded anxious. 'Plans? What plans are those? What are you going to do?'

He looked into my eyes and smiled as if he knew how I felt. 'Don't get so het up, Rachel! We all have plans for the future, don't we? I mean, you and your career which you'll be returning to . . . and me with mine.'

'But — ' I stuttered. ' — we can't have plans while Uncle is still unwell; while I'm here and you're here . . . I mean, everything must carry on just as it is . . . mustn't it?'

Ben took my hands in his and drew

me close to him. I remembered that wonderful kiss, and felt myself tremble. But my mind was too busy to allow the feelings to continue. I said, unsteadily, 'What are you trying to tell me, Ben?'

His voice was music again, resonating, making me wonder what magic he possessed to sound like this — quiet, reassuring, and memorable. It was the words that struck me so hard.

'I've been invited on another expedition, Rachel. My patron, Lord Blanchley, is keen to continue his plant hunting, and wants me to lead it for him. Not Asia this time, but a small island off the Russian coast — should be fascinating, and full of unknown exotics. I can't wait to go.'

My words came without thought, just full of emotion. 'You want to go! To leave here! But how can I manage this nursery without you? When we're beginning to get on so well . . . oh, Ben, I can't believe that you really mean to go!'

He frowned, looking disturbed but determined. 'Look, Rachel, you know I only came for a short while — just out of friendship, really — and already the days have flown past.'

My emotions slowly settled down. He was right. Time flew like a river in flood . . . And then suddenly I remembered. 'Uncle's op is tomorrow! I must go and see him this evening.'

'I'll come with you. After all, he offered me a two-week trial, didn't he?' A smile eased the tension from his face and helped me to calm down. 'I need to know if I passed the test, even though I shall be leaving quite soon.'

And so we parted friends again, but I had his plan running around my mind for the rest of the day.

We found Uncle Dexter in a cheerful mood, although I fancied his smile was forced, and his words trying to convince us how strong-minded he was. 'The great day approaches! I've waited long enough for it. Just think, in a day or two I shall know the worst — to walk again, or not!'

Ben and I exchanged glances, but

smiled brightly at Uncle. I said, 'Think positively, that always works! And we'll be doing the same. Ned and Katie sent their best wishes, Uncle, and will be along to see you once you're back again.'

He nodded, picked up the tiny posy I had brought him, and smelled the wonderful hyacinth fragrance. 'To be back in the nursery. That's my hope, Rachel, of course it is.' He turned to Ben, clearly trying to keep cheerful. 'And to see your exotics bed, my boy. How's it all growing?'

'Very well, sir, I'm glad to say. In particular, the blue wall covering is in bud, and I do believe there's a bud sprouting up in the Bird of Paradise plant. And I've had quite a few comments from visitors — good ones, too. Makes me believe that it was right to expand the business in this new way.'

Uncle nodded, and I saw his thoughts relaxing into his beloved garden. 'I think I offered you a two-week trial, Ben?'

Ben caught my eye, then looked back at Uncle. 'Yes, you did,' he said quietly.

'And I do hope I've passed your test — it's important to me to keep learning and gain experience, you see.'

Uncle looked at him, his eyes showing great interest. But then he looked across at me. 'I think the one to ask is Rachel, who has had to work with you and manage things. Well, Rachel, what's your opinion? Is Ben a hard-working business manager you have found helpful?'

I heard amusement in the last words, and then remembered how strongly I had been against employing Ben in the first place. I bowed my head. 'Uncle, I can only tell you that Ben has been wonderful. He's worked hard, helping both Ned and me when we were actually gardening . . . and then, in other ways, I've enjoyed having him around'.

My words were quiet, but my thoughts ran riot. For there were so many ways in which I had enjoyed his company — in particular, him finding all this amazing new information about Uncle's family. And very soon he would go. It was all a bit hard to take, and I looked the other way as I felt tears pricking at my eyelids.

I didn't know if Uncle — or Ben — realized how disturbed I was, but Uncle said, 'Well, it sounds as if you deserve a golden cup or something, Ben. Yes, I think you've passed your test very well. Congratulations!' He held out his hand and they shook, smiling at each other. Then Uncle added, his voice low and quiet, 'And thank you with all my heart for coming to the rescue with Rachel.' He looked at me. 'For, despite her strength and business knowledge, I do believe her when she says she values your help.'

The room settled into a silence which ran through me like a silver thread, knowing now that I indeed had feelings for Ben Hunter which would never leave me.

Then the familiar knock on the door, and enter Mrs Bond, looking even more authoritative than usual. 'Sorry to break up the party, but I do think Mr Swann needs an early night . . . ' And we were ushered out of the room with farewell hugs and kisses, and hopes for tomorrow flying high.

We walked back through the quiet village, and Ben reached for my hand. 'Thank you for saying kind things, Rachel,' he said, looking down through the dimpsey into my eyes. 'I know it's been a hard time for you, but we've come through, haven't we? I shall never forget being here at the nursery, with you.'

'Even when you're on this isolated island somewhere near Russia, pushing through giant undergrowth and getting excited about what you're finding?' I asked, dryly.

He drew me close, and put his hands about my face. 'Even then,' he whispered, and kissed my cheek. 'I shall be looking forward to coming home and finding you — wherever you are. And perhaps we can pick up the threads then — what do you think, Rachel?'

I pulled away. This was all too much:

Uncle's fears; Mrs Bond's orders; and now Ben, saying wonderful things but still planning to go away. I walked quickly back to the cottage, called 'Goodnight' over my shoulder, and went up to bed.

Dreams — oh yes, I had those — but not the ones I longed for.

14

Thursday, and everybody in the nursery was quiet, no doubt immersed in thoughts of Uncle Dexter. But we all worked that much harder, and I was thankful when Friday blew in with a breezy wind which set all the blossom flying.

Bryony and her gang of school-children appeared in good time, and at once we set to work. Gareth brought bamboo canes which he built into a neat small circle, firmly refusing any offers of help, while the other kids talked about spring onions, nasturtiums, and 'pretty pink daisies', and quiet Nina confided in me that she would like to grow a heart-shaped bed of marigolds for her Mum, asking me to help with it. And, of course, everybody expected the sunflowers to be showing! 'Next week,' I said hopefully.

Bryony came to me as the hour ended. 'I understand you'll be at Mrs Howarth Jones's party this evening,' she said, looking at me with keen eyes. 'Teddy and I will be there, of course . . .'

'Yes,' I said calmly, turning away and wondering if it was envy I saw on her face. 'Ben and I are looking forward to it, but I must think about the flower arrangements now — so excuse me running away.' And, as I waved goodbye to the children, I heard her say 'Ben?' as if she was very surprised.

I worked hard for the rest of the day, asking Ned and Rosemary to stand in for me for an hour during the lunch period while I picked my flowers. I enjoyed myself, wandering around the beds where all the lovely cottage garden plants were growing up towards the sunlight, secateurs in my hand, and images of the finished arrangements in my mind. At last they were all in buckets of cold water in the shade, having their fill before I could think about putting them in vases.

And then I phoned the hospital, enquiring about Uncle Dexter, to be told that the operation was successful and the patient feeling not too bad. No visitors today, which was a bit of a relief, as time was flying.

At teatime, I smiled at Ben, and said hopefully, 'Could you take my place for an hour before we close, Ben? I have to get the flowers arranged.'

At once he nodded and smiled back at me. 'That's fine, Rachel. Go and do your arrangements — and then I suggest you have a few minutes' rest before we set out for the great supper. By the way, I've ordered a taxi to take us and the flowers up to the Manor. Coming at quarter to seven — OK with you?'

I sighed with relief. 'That's wonderful. Giving me time to do the arrangements again when I get there — and no rush. Ben, how thoughtful you are!' I could have hugged him, but instead I walked away, forcing my mind into flower-arranging.

The kitchen was quiet as I put all my chosen vases onto the long scrubbed table and set to work. Each little pot was given a few green leaves which curled themselves around the actual vase, providing a firm base for the flowers. Fragrant white narcissus in the tallest pot, with a sprig of lime-green alexander from the hedge fanning out behind them, and then a couple of mauve hellebores. It looked lovely, I thought.

By the time I'd finished, I had homes for all the flowers I'd picked — scarlet geraniums, yellow tulips, purple honesty, white daises, and some blue rosemary; with sprays of cow parsley providing a delicate background. I put them all in a huge box and then went to dress myself up.

A rest, Ben had advised. So I lay on my bed and tried to clear my mind of everything except the fact that a good evening lay ahead, which I hoped we should all enjoy. Then I got up, showered, put on my new dress, brushed my hair until it shone, and looked in the mirror. There was a certain something about me, I thought — shining eyes, a smile not far away. Was it the prospect of a jolly evening? Or the flowers? Or being with Ben?

I went downstairs with a skip in my step and found him waiting in the kitchen, the big box of flowers ready to be carried out when the taxi arrived.

He looked at me as I came through the doorway. 'New dress? New *Rachel* — my word, you look glamorous!'

We laughed together, and I said, 'Thank you.' And then I really looked at him. Hair combed neatly behind his ears. And the new shirt which I had put on his bed with a thank-you note — well, there it was, on him, looking smart, the tiny check almost matching his green-blue eyes, which caught mine with what I felt was a special meaning.

I said, a bit nervously, 'You didn't mind about the shirt, Ben? I just wanted to say thank you, you see . . . '

He came closer, put his arms around me and gave me a hug which was warm and strong. 'No need for thanks, Rachel — working with you here in this wonderful place has been very enjoyable. I shall never forget it.'

Quickly, I stepped out of his embrace. Of course, he was going away, back to his adventurous life somewhere remote and far away from me. How could I forget?

And then the taxi man poked his head around the door. 'Ready to go to the Manor, Mr Hunter?'

The two men carried the box of flower arrangements out to the taxi, and Ben and I sat ourselves around it. It wasn't far to the Manor, and again they carried the box into the entrance, where Tessa Browning greeted us with a big smile.

'You're in good time,' she said. 'Mr Hunter, perhaps you'd like to walk around the garden while Rachel does her flowers? Supper isn't until eight o'clock, although we'll meet in the kitchen at a quarter to for drinks.'

Ben said he would very much like to wander in the gardens; the taxi left; and I was taken into the kitchen with my flower arrangements, then left alone.

I looked around me before doing anything — the kitchen was ultra-modern, all white paint and gleaming machinery, although the long stripped-pine table in the middle was old and welcoming, and I knew at once that my small vases with their brilliant flowers and greenery would make a huge impact on the modernism all around me.

I was happily lost for some time — watering, rearranging, standing back and admiring what I had done — until a familiar voice sounded behind me. 'Rache! My word, look at you! All dressed up. And in the middle of your flowers. Well, this looks like being a good party, doesn't it?'

Teddy Walters, with Bryony behind him, staring at me without a smile on her face.

I turned slowly. 'Yes, I'm sure it will be very enjoyable. Excuse me, I must go into the garden and find Ben — it's nearly time for drinks to be served, I believe . . . See you in a minute.'

I made my escape through the door leading onto the terrace. But I heard Teddy's sarcastic voice saying to Bryony, 'So, she's with that rough chap, is she? Hope he knows how to dress for a civilized party.'

I thought, then, how right had been my decision to break with Teddy — he definitely wasn't the right man for me. But perhaps Bryony found him attractive? *Well, good for her*, I told myself as I went looking for Ben.

The supper party proved most enjoyable. Mrs Howarth Jones, resplendent in a bright blue dress with gold jewellery all over her, was welcoming and friendly; and told me, when we had finished eating and were into the coffee stage, that my flower arrangements had really enhanced the lovely white kitchen.

'My dear,' she boomed, 'you are so

talented. I shall let my friends see what you have done, and I'm sure they will be delighted to give you commissions in future. I can see your beautiful nursery becoming quite famous!'

Then she sat down beside Ben, and got him to tell her amazing tales of hacking down thick and almost unpassable greenery in order to get at one particular plant and bring it back to England. Which made my thoughts start pushing together into a painful mess. Ben going away, and me returning to London and Beautiful Bunches. And Uncle Dexter? I didn't know. But how complicated life had suddenly become!

The evening drew on, and we still chatted and laughed, looking at the Manor garden — serene and beautiful in the moonlight, with bats flying about and a blackbird singing in the distance. And then it was time to go.

Teddy and Bryony paused by his car, and he called to us — 'Want a lift home, Rache?'

I shook my head and glanced at Ben. He looked relieved when I called back, 'No, thanks. It's not far to walk.'

So Ben and I left the Manor behind us and walked along the quiet lane; not speaking, but — at least in my case — trying to cope with churning thoughts.

When we reached the nursery entrance, Ben stopped, looked at the school garden, and then grinned at me. 'I'd say Swann's Nursery is undergoing quite a few changes, Rachel — children's favourites, exotic plants, and home-grown herbs — what do you think about it?'

I took a minute to reply. The sunflowers were now showing — big green shoots in the rich soil. The kids would be so pleased. Then I said, slowly, 'Yes, lots of changes. And they affect us all, don't they? You going off to find more plants — me wondering about taking commissions for flowers here, or going back to London. And all of it depending on how Uncle Dexter is . . . '

We stood there in the cool moonlight, looking at each other, until Ben said very quietly: 'I told you I shall be coming back to find you, Rachel. But I have to go. It's my career, can you understand?'

I nodded. Of course I could. Careers were what we all thought about and planned for. How could one change one's needs? It didn't seem possible. So I said simply, 'Yes, Ben, I understand. You're off to goodness knows where; and once Uncle Dexter is back, I shall return to a small flat in London, working at my chosen business. That's how our lives are working out — we can't change them, can we?'

His arms went around me: warm, strong, reassuring, and what I needed so badly. I heard him whisper, 'I wonder . . . ' as he lifted my face towards him.

A kiss. Another kiss, pleasure racing through me, and new hope. Could we change everything?

But then I drew away from him. Wonderful kisses were no guarantee of a happy, settled future, were they?

I stepped out of his arms, saw the

disappointment in his eyes, but knew I was doing the right thing. We were both soon to part, and go our separate ways. Loving must be just a memory.

I took in a deep breath, ran towards the cottage door and then glanced back.

'Goodnight, Ben,' I said. 'Thanks for everything. Must go to bed now . . . ' And I closed the door behind me.

Dreams again, muddled and unsettling. I was glad to wake next morning and firmly tell myself, *This is a new day. Take it as it comes.* And went downstairs with a very determined smile on my face.

★ ★ ★

Rosemary came into the nursery during the weekend, and asked me if I had a few minutes to spare. 'I want to talk to you about something, Rachel . . . '

The expression on her face told me it was important. At once, I put aside what I was doing, and led her into the tunnel where there were only young plants to hear our conversation.

'It's about the nursery, and the Swann family,' she said, as we found stools and sat down facing each other.

Knowing what Ben had found out, I was intrigued. 'Tell me,' I said quickly.

She blinked, and then took a steadying breath. 'I think I told you I vaguely recalled something about the name Swann. Well, I've remembered a bit more now. And I found some old papers — a letter from an aunt of mine to a relative of hers, called Swann.'

Now it was my turn for the steadying breath. 'Yes, Rosemary? Please go on.'

She looked at me very intently, and a slow smile framed her face. 'Rachel, we are related. Can you believe it? And I've worked out that your Uncle Dexter is a distant cousin of mine.' She fumbled in a pocket for her hanky, and wiped her face. But the smile remained, overwhelming the rush of emotion.

I got off my stool and went to her side, bending to put my arms around

196

her. 'Rosemary, I did know this. Ben searched online and found the details, and we were waiting to tell you next time you came to work here. But you've told me instead now!'

'Yes,' she said tremulously. 'And so I want you to come with me to the hospital, and see your uncle and tell him too. But I'm a bit nervous — how will he take such extraordinary news?'

I sat down again and thought. Then I said, 'I believe he will be tremendously pleased at being in touch with his forgotten family again. You see, he's a lonely man, and of course he's worried about the result of the operation. Tell you what, Rosemary, shall we go this afternoon and visit him? And tell him he has a new distant cousin? Surely that will be the most cheering news possible!' I smiled at her, and was glad to see her smile back: serenely, and — I thought — hopefully.

'That will be wonderful, Rachel,' she said. 'We can catch the bus into town, and then it's only a short walk to the hospital.' She rose, tucked her hanky back into her pocket and walked to the entrance of the tunnel where she turned, looked at me, and gave me a smile I knew I would always remember. Very quietly and steadily, she said, 'Life often gives one the most wonderful gifts, doesn't it?'

And, as I followed her out into the sunlight and the busy stream of customers, I knew that what she had just said was very true indeed.

15

We found Uncle Dexter sitting up in bed, holding court with various visitors; and smiling a big welcome at us as we appeared. The other visitors said goodbye, and Rosemary and I were left at his bedside.

I felt a little nervous, having to introduce Rosemary and then explain, but to my surprise she took the lead — holding out her hand towards him, smiling, and saying quietly, in her calm, steady voice, 'Mr Swann, Rachel and I have discovered that I have a connection with your family in the past. Would you be interested enough for me to tell you about it?'

Uncle looked amazed. His gaze switched from her to me, and I smiled reassuringly. 'It's such good news, Uncle, I think you'll be very pleased.'

Slowly, he nodded; pointed at the

chairs and waited until we were seated; then said in his deep voice, 'All right. Let's hear about it.'

On the bus journey there, Rosemary and I had discussed how we would present the extraordinary facts. So I began, as we had arranged, with Great-Aunt Georgina, telling Uncle about her abandoned baby and its life through the ongoing years. I watched his expression, saw it grow unbelieving, and then nodded at Rosemary to finish the story.

She took it up quietly, making it sound almost ordinary. 'Yes, Mr Swann, the baby survived, and had a family which also lived on — finally leaving me as a present-day, rather forgotten, member of your family.' She stopped and smiled at Uncle, whose eyes were wide with wonder. Then she added simply, 'Mr Swann, I think we are very distant cousins.'

There was a heavy silence in the warm, airless little room, until Uncle stirred.

'A story I never thought to hear. But one that — why, yes — pleases me beyond words. So you, Mrs Leach — '

'Rosemary, please.'

'Of course. So we are cousins, you and I — and my name is Dexter.' He held out both hands, and I was very moved to see how gladly she put hers into his grasp.

They sat there, looking at each other, and I felt tears pricking behind my eyelids. And then a trolley came into the room.

'Tea?' asked the trolley lady, and we all smiled with relief and said yes, please.

After all that emotion, it was good to calm down and to hear Uncle's news about his operation. 'Successful,' he said heartily, with a huge smile. 'Can't say when I shall be walking, but no reason to think I shan't be able to — just have to exercise and be patient. Wonderful, isn't it?'

Rosemary and I sighed with relief. 'Wonderful, Uncle,' I echoed. 'So you'll be back in the nursery before we know it!'

His big smile faded a little. 'Give me time, Rachel, dear child,' he said quietly. 'One is never quite sure about the future, eh?'

I nodded, realizing the truth of those words.

Then Rosemary said — as steadily as usual, but with such a warm tone to her voice that I sat back, surprised — 'And where will you be, Cousin Dexter, whilst waiting for your future to show itself?'

I watched his face tighten. After a moment, he sighed, and said, 'I shall stay at the Fairwater Valley Hotel, I imagine. I can't possibly inflict myself — still an invalid — on my old home, Swann Cottage in the nursery. I must simply wait and see.'

Rosemary nodded, and I guessed from her expression that an idea was running through her mind. But she said no more; and soon, seeing that Uncle Dexter was looking tired, I suggested we leave, to return soon.

He managed a smile. 'I'm expecting

to leave here in two days' time, so you won't have to keep making that tiresome journey to see me. I'll be back in the village.'

Our eyes met, and he twinkled a bit. 'Back with Mrs Bond. Well, we'll see.'

We got to our feet and made our goodbyes. At the door, he called me back. 'Rachel, where's that young man, Ben? I'd like to see him, to talk about those exotics he's growing.'

I felt myself stiffen, and my smile died. 'I'll tell him, Uncle, but any day now he'll be off on a new expedition. Somewhere around the coast of Russia this time.'

Uncle's face eased a bit. 'Interesting. A pity he's leaving — he's helpful and knowledgeable. And I've been thinking quite a lot about expanding that one bed of his . . . ' He smiled at me. 'You'll miss him, Rachel. But now you've got Rosemary to help, no doubt the work will still be done.'

Rosemary and I agreed in chorus, and then waved goodbye as we left his room. But my mind settled on Ben and his new expedition as we sat in the bus on the way back to the village. Yes, I certainly would miss him . . .

But then I decided to stop thinking about him, and instead get down to creating a flower arrangement for the competition. *Handsome and Out of the Ordinary* — the words happily filled my mind, and I was smiling when eventually we walked into the nursery and found Katie busy with the teapot.

Ben asked about the state of the patient, and I told him what Uncle Dexter had told me.

'He'd like to see me? That's great. I'll go tomorrow, if you don't mind me sneaking off on the bus after lunch?'

I turned away from him. 'We'll manage somehow,' I said dryly. 'After all, you won't be here much longer, will you?'

I got on with my work. I felt he wanted to say something to make matters right, but he just stood there for a moment or two, and then muttered, 'All right. If that's how you feel . . . '

With that, he marched away, intent on doing something in the tunnel.

Uncle had talked about his future, and I thought and thought about mine. It seemed that he might well return to the nursery — although how much work he could physically do, I wasn't sure. And then I had to consider returning to Beautiful Bunches when my two-month sabbatical was up. It seemed not quite the happy future I had once thought.

What on earth was the matter with me? I delved into flower-arranging ideas as quickly as I could, slowly working out a list of possible candidates growing here in the nursery. As the list grew, I found that my mind relaxed. Even Ben's leaving not seeming to matter so much.

The days passed, and so did the weeks. Uncle Dexter returned to the hotel, and obediently followed his doctor's advice to relax, but to exercise, too. We all visited him, but it was Rosemary who managed to bring a smile to his face, and even to make him laugh. I wondered at the friendly relationship building between them, and was grateful for Rosemary's obviously growing affection for her newfound second cousin. And for the fact that Uncle Dexter was, daily, growing lighter-hearted and happier.

Ben told me he had visited Uncle, and they had discussed the idea of expanding the one exotic bed that he had planted. 'Told me he was thinking of buying up that set-aside field just up the road, making it into a properly exotic garden — if I thought enough customers were interested enough to buy from it. I said, why not? Take a chance, hope for the best. And I would be glad to advise about new plants.'

Just in time, I stopped myself from saying, *But you won't be here*, because now that we were talking again without any problems, I didn't want anything to go wrong. So I smiled, nodded, and asked if he had seen the wonderful delphiniums growing in the long border.

'I might use a couple in my competition flower arrangement,' I mused, and suddenly he looked interested.

'I'd forgotten about that, Rachel — sorry! Getting it all ready, are you? When's the entry date?'

'Middle of next week. I'll have to get a move on, because it'll take a while to see exactly how I want to arrange my flowers, and to find a suitable container.'

He smiled, and I knew we were friends again. 'Rachel, when you've got it all done, why don't we have an evening out? A meal at the pub? Or another picnic by the river? Up to you.'

'A picnic,' I said, without further thought. 'That would be lovely, Ben, thank you.'

We arranged to have the picnic on Friday evening, a date Ben picked, saying that it would be a good end to the week. I agreed.

I managed to fit in thoughts on the competition while working in the nursery — and, yes, more and more people seemed to be interested in the huge exotics. They were now growing well, and those that flowered were producing buds.

Sitting down with a much-needed mug of tea under the cypress tree, with five minutes to spend on my own thoughts, I went through the list of flowers I had decided would make my competition entry Out of the Ordinary — and, I hoped, truly Handsome. The hedge-banks at the far end of the nursery were rich in wildflowers; some of these, I knew, would fit in with my more domesticated blooms. Spurge, for instance — lime-green, very large and blowsy — would be a wonderful foil for the elegant, deep-purple iris heads I had growing in the summer border. Some yellow Welsh poppies would take the flower range even further, and then I would soften and structure the whole arrangement with delicate cow parsley and bright green fern leaves, all holding a small, bright ruff of forget-me-nots. Of course, it would then need one large flower which would surprise viewers even more . . .

I was still trying to decide what that would be — a wild purple orchid, perhaps — when Ben found me there and sat down, smiling. 'Two minutes I can spare, and that's it. I can see one of my interested exotic customers heading for the bed, and I must be there. Just to remind you, Rachel, of our date this evening. Fish and chips again?'

I returned the smile. 'Lovely. And I know a different spot where we can sit and eat. Might even see a kingfisher! Seven o'clock?'

He stood up, saluted. 'Yes, Miss. I'll be there.' And strode back to his waiting customer and the exotic bed.

Rosemary was about to leave the Nursery at the usual time of five-thirty, but stood waiting by the office door as I came towards her. 'Rachel, I wonder if we might have a word — can you spare a moment?'

I stopped. 'Of course. Come in here ... ' Was it something about working here? Was it getting too much for her? Or might it be about Uncle Dexter? My heart started to pound.

We said goodnight to Ned, who was just leaving, and then sat down, looking at each other.

'Well?' I asked nervously.

She smiled, and her serene, reassuring expression at once helped settle my uneasiness.

'Not a great worry, Rachel, but something that needs attention, as I see it. Dexter — ' And here she actually blushed, speaking his name. ' — Dexter and Mrs Bond are having arguments, and I believe he is wanting to leave the hotel. What do you think?'

I thought hard. Yes, it sounded important that he should move somewhere else, away from that awkward — yet kindly, if strong-minded — Mrs Bond. Somewhere quiet in the village, perhaps — I knew he wouldn't return to Swann Cottage yet. Living on his own? But what if he couldn't cope with such a life? Perhaps he needed a carer? Oh no, not Uncle Dexter, with his determination to walk again and his growing energy! But someone who could be there for him; someone who might give him peace and new happiness . . .

I stared at Rosemary, and saw she

shared my thoughts. 'Well,' I stumbled, 'what do you mean, exactly? What are you suggesting?'

She retained her composure, but her eyes were brighter than usual. 'You don't know how big my cottage is, do you, Rachel? I think you've only seen it from the outside. Actually, it's quite large — with an empty bedroom which, at the moment, I fill with junk because I haven't got round to sorting everything out. But . . . ' Her smile glowed. ' . . . I was thinking of offering the room — cleared out, of course — to Dexter. The cottage is quiet, at the end of the village; it has a garden he could look at and sit in — and perhaps tidy up, once he gets his legs working — and . . . ' She stopped, smiled at me even more radiantly, and whispered, 'And I should so love to have him there.'

Something inside me glowed and warmed me. What a good woman she was; and how lovely if this new distant-cousin relationship proved beneficial for both of them. Instantly, I could envision Uncle

Dexter padding about in her garden, his mind once again on plants, in a setting which could only do him immense good. And within reach of his beloved nursery, if fate allowed him to walk again in the near future.

I cleared my throat, blinked away threatening tears, and smiled back at her.

'I can't think of anything better,' I told her. 'Shall we go and see Uncle this evening, and see what he thinks? Oh, Rosemary, I do hope he agrees!'

16

Uncle Dexter was sitting in the chair beside his bed. He looked brighter and altogether better, and greeted us with his famous warm smile. 'Lovely to see you! Come and sit somewhere — on the bed, perhaps. Things are looking up, and although this chair is hard, I'm glad to be in it and feeling more alive!'

Of course we told him how delighted we were, and I asked when he might be leaving the hospital.

'One more day. Looking forward to leaving very much.' And then his expression changed. 'No doubt Mrs Bond will be glad to see me back. I just hope she won't start ordering me about again. Well, I shan't put up with it. I'm much more myself now, and I intend to be the one giving the orders!'

'As usual, Uncle,' I said with a wry smile, and he laughed aloud.

'How well you know me, Rachel, my dear. But perhaps I'll get softer as I grow older!'

Rosemary bent forward and touched his arm. 'Don't change, Cousin Dexter,' she said quietly, and smiled. 'But until you reach that far-away old age, I have a suggestion to make, which might — and I do hope it does — please you.'

'Really?' Uncle Dexter looked at her with an expression of wonder. 'Well, let's hear it.'

'That you become a lodger in my cottage, at least until you want to go elsewhere. I have a spare bedroom, I can cook reasonably well, and my garden needs a firm hand. Please, cousin, think about it. You could be quiet, yet part of the village, and not very far from the nursery.' She stopped, and I saw her smile growing. 'And I would love to have you as my lodger.'

Silence as we all looked at each other with traces of emotion on our faces. Uncle bowed his head for a moment, then looked up again, and smiled at Rosemary.

'What have I done to deserve such a

kind offer?' he said very quietly. And then — 'I'm inclined to say yes at once, but I know I need to think about it. Dear Cousin Rosemary, will you allow me a day or two in which to decide?'

'However long it takes.' She removed her hand and gave him that steady, calm smile. 'But I shall live in hope!'

I thought the little room had a new, happier atmosphere as we continued to sit there and chat, until it was time for Uncle to get out of the chair and start his physical exercises. We left him looking very bright, waving at us as we made our way out of the room and down the corridor.

'Give me a few days,' he called after us. 'Come and see me then, and I'll have the answer ready!'

Day after day passed, as they do, and I knew that I must start on my competition entry. Monday was usually a quiet time with few customers, so I told Ned I would take an hour off to pick my flowers.

He nodded and grinned. 'Heard that

the Manor lady was really pleased with the ones you did for her supper, Miss Rachel.'

A glow spread inside me. I did so enjoy arranging flowers — well, I supposed that soon I would be back in London doing just that every day. And then I frowned. How could I be sure about it? At the moment, life seemed a bit precarious — I wasn't sure what might happen next. If Uncle Dexter was unable to come back to the nursery, I couldn't just go off and leave him. And with Ben going . . .

Quickly, I stopped thinking about that. I picked up my basket and secateurs, strode down to the far end of the nursery where the wildflowers grew, and started cutting.

The sight of those delicate flowers nodding in the breeze lightened my spirits as I walked back towards the cottage, put my selections into a bucket of water, and left them to recover from their picking. I was so pleased to see that my ideas of colour and structure seemed to be working. Tomorrow I would find just the right container, and then arrange them.

Ned called me into the office as I went off on the next job. 'Phone call, Miss Rachel.'

I was surprised to hear Tessa Browning's voice, warm and friendly. 'Hi, Rachel, sorry to interrupt your work, but I have a message for you. One of Mrs Haworth Jones's friends has asked me to contact you. Are you still doing flower arrangements? Because if so, she would like you to see her to talk about an important event next month, for which she wants some of your work. Shall I give you her name and number?'

Surprise mixed with worry spread through me. 'Tessa, I'm a bit confused at the moment — not sure if I shall still be here then — though I suppose I might be . . . ' I stopped. The idea of doing more flower arrangements was wonderful, but I really had no idea about my immediate future. Here, or back in London?

But eventually I realized I was being very unbusinesslike, so said firmly, 'Thank you so much, Tessa. Yes, of course I'll contact whoever it is, and make arrangements to do what she wants.' *Well*, I thought, *I suppose, if I'm back in London, I could come down for a weekend and do it all . . .*

She gave me the name and address, and then we chatted for a few moments. 'Busy?' she asked, and I smiled as I answered, 'Very busy. Everything is going well. Why don't you drop by, Tessa, and I could treat you to a cup of coffee and a look at all our beautiful flowers that are growing so well?' I laughed. 'Don't worry, you won't have to buy anything!'

'Thanks, Rachel — I would love to. Perhaps next week?'

'Fine. Look forward to seeing you. Cheers . . . '

I put down the receiver and went on my way. And it struck me suddenly, and with a feeling of pleasure, that I had friends here in the village. But in London? Mere acquaintances who were only interested in selling their arrangements. I must make up my mind what to do.

That evening, I spent a long time finding a container for my prize flowers; a pewter-coloured, plain, bucket-shaped vase that would not detract from the flowers' palette. With the experience I had gained over my three years in London creating arrangements, I had no difficulty.

And I thought, at the end of the evening, as I cleared away chopped-off stems and stripped leaves, that this was a very good one. I felt proud of it — and yet, as I took it to the cold frame where it could spend the night, I knew something was missing. It needed a special, colourful flower to pull all the other pieces together and declare that this was something definitely Handsome — and even Out of the Ordinary, too.

I stood in the shadowy garden and thought hard; but the only flower that came to mind was the one beautiful, tall, purple wild orchid I had seen growing in the middle of the bluebells in the old woodland. Well, that would have to do. Tomorrow I would go and pick it, then photograph my completed arrangement and send it off to London and the competition people.

But the next morning was suddenly so busy, what with early customers and then the schoolchildren arriving, that I forgot about the orchid and the arrangement. I told myself it could wait another day, that nothing would harm it until I had more time to finish it off.

So I joked with Gareth, listened to Nina's thoughts about her mother's birthday next week, encouraged the children to look after the seeds that had now germinated and needed looking after. Some weeding went on, with occasional mistakes which had to be replanted quickly and then watered; and when Bryony finally came up to me as the hour finished, I said, 'It's going well, isn't it? I hope Teddy's pleased about it?'

Her pretty face clouded. 'I wouldn't know. He's off on a new scheme now, looking for someone who can talk to the kids about emails and apps — I think he's forgotten the garden here.'

I felt sorry for her, but recalled that that was just how Teddy was when I first knew him; always rushing off after new things.

'I'm sorry, Bryony,' I said, and she nodded at me, trying to smile as she said lightly, 'Plenty more fish in the sea, eh? I'm not bothered. But, yes, I am so pleased with how this garden grows — all thanks to you, Rachel.'

'Not just me, Bryony, but Mr Swann, and Ned, and the enthusiasm of the children themselves.'

Bryony started chivvying the children to clear up, ready to go back to school. But she added, 'It's doing so much good. Gareth says he will be a gardener when he grows up, and Nina has started writing poetry about her flowers . . . Well, cheerio, Rachel; see you next week.' And off the group went, chattering and giggling down the road with Bryony in the midst of them.

A successful project, I thought

gratefully, and returned to one of the many jobs awaiting me in the nursery, thinking that I must tell Uncle Dexter this when I visited him after lunch.

He was sitting in his chair, upright, and smiling, and clearly waiting to see me. 'Rachel, dear child, so here you are. Tell me the nursery news, and then I'll tell you mine.'

I think I knew from that smile, and the feeling of excitement that ran through him, what his news would be; but I obediently recounted all that had happened at the nursery in the last few days. The school garden; the selling of many plants to visiting customers; my news about a new flower commission; and, finally, the prize arrangement which I was quite proud of. 'It just needs a final flower, and then it's done. I can send the photo off and then just wait and see. But now, Uncle, don't keep me waiting any longer — what is your news?'

He sat back, very straight and smiling, and looked at me with an expression of amused pleasure. 'Mrs Bond wasn't at all pleased when I said I might leave. In fact, I fear we had a bit of a set-to. She reminded me of all she had done for me, which I gratefully acknowledged, but her attitude made me all the more determined to leave here.'

We looked at each other very directly. His smile faded, and his voice quietened into that steely one which I remembered from his direction of work at the nursery. 'Rachel, I have taken Rosemary's kind offer of accommodation, and will be moving very soon. I have written to tell her, to say how grateful I am, and how I look forward to being her lodger.'

I nodded, and said, quietly, 'I'm delighted, Uncle. And I know you've made the right decision.' A pause, and then I added, 'How shall we go about moving you? I'm sure Ned and Ben will help — and, of course, so will Rosemary and I.'

He chuckled. 'No need, dear child. I have friends in the village — remember Jim Buckley, who runs that small Helping Hand business? I've asked him to come round and arrange it for me.'

Well! So everything seemed to be done! How pleased I was. I stayed for another five minutes, and then said I must get back to work. We parted with a warm embrace, and Uncle's promise to ask if there was anything I could do. I left him smiling to himself, no doubt making plans for the move.

Downstairs I met Mrs Bond who looked at me without a smile, and said coldly, 'So your uncle is going. I suppose this is all your doing, Miss Swann. Well, I only hope he'll be all right. For he certainly won't get the attention he has had here.'

I had only one answer. 'You may be right about that, Mrs Bond, but he will be receiving a lot of love, and that's the important thing.'

I left her standing with a strange look on her face, but put that to the back of my mind as I hurried along to the nursery. For now I was thinking about my evening out with Ben — another picnic, and I knew just the place to take him to.

17

It was perfect in the grove, down by the river. A small space I had discovered when an angry teenager, needing to be alone to brood on the faults of people and the world. Now it was just peace I found there — and Ben, with a picnic in his backpack.

'Fish and chips again?' I asked as we looked for places to sit.

He grinned, and put his jacket over a likely-looking stone for me. 'Certainly not. A new shop in the village that does burgers with salad garnish. Does that appeal to you, madam?'

'Mmm. Sounds very good. Well done, Ben.'

With him bracing his back against a birch tree-trunk, and me on the rock, we started our picnic. And yes, it was a good one. Water from the river to wash it down . . . and then just quietness as we watched the flow and dance of the river, and listened to the birds in the trees bordering it.

When the picnic was finished, I looked at Ben, and knew I had to say something that was running around my mind. But it wouldn't be easy.

'Ben — ' I stopped because he had turned to look at me, and the expression on his face made me wonder what he was thinking. Somehow I faced the challenge, and found the words.

'Do you really have to leave the nursery, Ben? Is this new expedition so important to you?'

I watched him thinking, and then he put a hand out to find mine. 'Yes, it is, Rachel. A big step up in my career as a plant collector, if that's what I want — and yes, I do want it. I know it's going to be hard to leave the nursery — I've enjoyed being with you and Ned, and getting to know your Uncle and Rosemary — but it's time to go. I have to move on.'

We looked into each other's eyes, and

I felt the warmth of his hand around mine. But my heart was cold and dispirited. So, even after the kisses we had shared, and our growing friendship, I knew the end had come.

I slipped my hand out of his and stared down at the slow-flowing river. 'I see.' And, yes, I did. His career meant everything to him, and I was just a pleasant, temporary part of his life, soon to fade away and become just a memory.

It was hard to accept that. To know that my cold heart would take a long while to warm up again . . . but that was what life did. And I knew I must be strong and begin the long search for happiness once more.

'I see,' I said again, and now I was able to smile at him, despite the coldness inside.

He put an arm around my shoulder and drew me closer.

'Rachel,' he said very quietly, with all the old music in his deep voice, 'I shall never forget you. And perhaps we might meet again? Sometime, when I'm back in England? Could you wait for me?'

What could I say? His arm was warm, and I knew that I longed to be even closer to him, feeling the beat of his heart, but it wasn't to be.

I drew away and got to my feet, saying briskly, 'Well, perhaps, who knows? And anyway, I have my own career to think about. I might return to my job in London — or do something else completely. I don't know yet.'

He was up, standing beside me, packing dirty plates and papers into his backpack. And now it was him saying, 'I see,' which helped me understand that we had reached an impasse which couldn't be resolved right now.

'Let's go back,' I said as brightly as I could manage. 'Maybe we'll see the kingfisher as we go. It always used to be here.'

'Things change,' Ben said, and I could only agree.

But we did see a flash of turquoise wings, and heard a high little call as the bird flashed down the river. And as we headed for the village and the nursery, we managed to chat quite easily about various subjects: the prize competition; Uncle Dexter moving in with Rosemary, the plans to grow more exotic plants . . .

We reached the entrance, admired the sunflowers, and then went on, finally stopping at the door to Swann Cottage. We looked at each other, and then he put his arms around me, and kissed both my cheeks.

'Thanks for a good evening,' he said. 'I shall remember it. And now to bed, I suppose?'

I nodded. 'I'm quite weary,' I said; and he replied, very quietly, 'I'll just have a wander down the garden.' Again, that look into my eyes, and then: 'Sleep well, Rachel.'

I did eventually sleep, but not well. Too many thoughts, too many muddling dreams. I was glad to wake with the dawn and decided to get up at once. My flower arrangement needed to be finished and photographed.

Outside, the air was deliciously cool, and I went to the cold frame to find my flowers, satisfaction running through me. They would be fine, ready now for the finishing touch — which I supposed must be the tall purple orchid, still growing down in the hedge.

But inside the cold frame was a strange, wonderful flower — Ben's Bird of Paradise, its head pushing up into the sky, and the vivid orange of those huge petals — in a glass of water, with a note propped against it.

I took a deep breath, opened the note and read it.

Rachel, can't say goodbye, it hurts too much. But I have to go. Please win the prize with this flower — and remember me. Ben.

I had to read it twice to understand that this was final. He had gone. And left me his adored flower.

It was hard to come to terms with this, and I lingered in the garden for a long time until Katie called me in for breakfast. I went in to think about porridge and toast and coffee, and wondered where he was, until I decided such thoughts were of no use. What mattered next was getting my flower arrangement into the best structure I could manage, then photographing it and sending the image off to London and the judges.

I did just that, and found my mind was able to revive slightly as I gazed at the various blooms, knowing that it was, indeed, Handsome. Because Ben's flower just finished off the beauty of the final arrangement — and even, I told myself hopefully, made it Out of the Ordinary. Well, I could only wait now, and try to get on with my lonely life.

It was great to walk through the village that evening and call on Rosemary — and Uncle Dexter. The Helping Hands van had done its business efficiently and well, and now there he was, sitting on the sunlit terrace with a drink on the table beside him, while Rosemary went in and out of the cottage, bringing with her the scent of something special in the cooking line.

They made me so welcome that I felt my heart slowly start to warm up again. I didn't mention Ben, but just told them I had finished my flower arrangement and sent the photo off to London. 'How long before you hear the results?' asked Uncle. I said it would be at least a week. And then he smiled and leaned forward in his chair. 'You're looking tired, dear child — it worries me. All the work you have had to do while I've been away . . . I think you need a change. Why not have a few days away from the nursery? Rosemary tells me she would like to work longer hours now, so you shouldn't worry about the jobs being done. Remember, a change is as good as a rest. Where would you like to go?'

I didn't answer at once, but felt warmth grow inside me at the idea — for, yes, it would be a good change to leave flowers for a few days, not to have to worry about too much work, and especially not to remember Ben. After a minute or two, I smiled at Uncle, and said, 'That's a lovely idea, Uncle, thank you. I should love to have a few days off — and I know just where I would like to go.'

Uncle smiled. 'Splendid! And where will that be?'

'London,' I said at once, with a lightening of my spirits. 'London, to visit my old job in Beautiful Bunches, and then go to Kew.'

Uncle nodded, and said, 'A wonderful place, but let's give it its proper name, shall we? The Royal Botanic Gardens of Kew!' And his smile grew.

Rosemary came in and sat down next to Uncle. She looked at me curiously. 'And what part of Kew will you be visiting, Rachel? It should all look wonderful in this lovely spring weather.'

I heard my voice grow lighter and brighter. 'I want to visit the pavilion where the lady plant collectors' paintings are on show. You see, I need to see just what Great-Aunt Georgina did, because then perhaps I can make up my mind about the future.'

A small, somewhat bemused silence, then Uncle asked lightly: 'Not planning to do what she did, are you? I think arranging flowers is much more in your line, my dear, than plunging through tropical forests dressed in a corset!'

'No — I think I would prefer to work in the nursery — oh, I don't know, but I think I shall find out if I go up there.'

'Fine,' said Uncle Dexter. 'I've got a brochure about Kew somewhere in the office — I can't get there myself yet, but if you have a good look, you'll find it. So start making your arrangements, dear child.' And then Rosemary was up, back in the kitchen, and telling us that supper was laid out in the little dining room next door. 'Rachel, please help Cousin Dexter with his crutches, will you?'

I spent the afternoon in the nursery: talking to customers; seeing how interested some of them were in Ben's tropical plants; and generally helping Ned with the million small jobs that always lay in wait for us. In the evening, I strolled down to the river and sat on my rock, thinking about me and about Ben.

I remembered our last conversation; I thought about him and his career, and then turned to my own indecision about what my future might hold. And with the song of the flowing water, and a blackbird whistling his favourite tune not far away, I was at last able to think sensibly and seriously, without too many emotions clouding my mind.

Make a list of pros and cons, I told myself. And this was what emerged: I loved the countryside deeply, and wished I would never have to live in a city again. And the commissions that seemed to be coming my way here. Flower arranging, I loved, too. A smile came as I thought about Uncle Dexter and Rosemary, and I knew that I loved them, and was loved in return. A big pro, that was.

And finally, who would run the nursery if Uncle never came back? I could do it; I had proved I could.

Then I tallied up the points against all that: which included my high-powered job in London waiting for me; the absence of Ben; the need to make a new life . . . Lastly, did I really want to bury myself in the countryside for ever? I was young — surely I needed a brighter lifestyle?

All these confusing thoughts churned around in my mind as I left the rock and sauntered back to the nursery. The school garden was green with emerging growth, and the sunflowers climbed an inch or two daily up the entrance posts. It dawned on me that one day, when they were older, Gareth — and perhaps Nina — might like to come and work here for a few hours each week. That would resolve the future labour question.

By the time the shadows told me it was bedtime, I knew I was on my own, but I had a cleared mind. And I knew the last factor in my decision would be the visit to Kew. In the morning, I would go and find the brochure Uncle had said was in his desk.

*   *   *

Scrutinising the brochure, I wondered at the pictures it brought with it. Why had I never visited this amazing place before? Well, I would go very soon!

I started planning dates, and the days flew past until Monday of next week arrived, and I caught the early train to London. I was on my way into my future.

The Gardens at Kew were alive with colour and plants. Trees, shrubs, the different houses where I could look at water lilies and sensitive tropical plants. I was thrown into a whirl of pleasure as I made my way through such treasures, heading for the pavilion where the prints of the paintings by the famous plant collector Marianne North were displayed. I spent a long time there, wondering at her talent, and then looked hopefully for a mention of Great-Aunt Georgina.

And she was there. Just one name among a list of other women collectors, but it was enough for me. She had been one of that strong band of Edwardian and Victorian ladies who broke free of their restrictive domestic lives. I felt so proud of her.

As I headed out of the Gardens, back towards the late train to take me back to the village, I was overflowing with pride about her. It brought with it a new feeling about how Ben needed to do just what she had done.

Slowly, then, I realized that, as a modern woman, I, too, could do whatever I wanted. And with a flash of insight, I knew what that was. My future suddenly lay ahead of me. It was all quite clear.

18

My first job, I decided, was to confirm all my thoughts of last night. For, of course, I intended to stay here at the nursery.

So I had to tender my resignation from the waiting job at Beautiful Bunches. I phoned them — a little nervously, for the managing director, Elizabeth, was known to be a strong character, and I wondered how she would receive my news.

I needn't have worried. 'Rachel!' she said with a friendly note in her strident voice. 'Good to hear from you. When are you coming back to us? We've missed you badly, you know.'

My confidence grew, and I said firmly, 'That's very nice of you, Elizabeth, but I fear I shan't be returning after all. You see, everything down here has changed, and I am taking over the managing of our family nursery. Sorry, but that's how it has to be. So please accept my resignation from Beautiful Bunches — I have enjoyed working with you, and learning so much . . . '

A slight pause, and then, 'I see. Well, good luck, Rachel, and I hope you will continue with your flower-arranging — we all thought you had a big talent for it. Yes, I have no option but to accept your resignation — but do keep in touch, won't you? And come and see us if you're in town any day.'

We chatted on for a few minutes, then ended the call, and I sighed with relief. Things were going the right way.

Next, I had to call the telephone number Tessa had given me regarding another flower arrangement. This too, ended happily, with a request for a wall installation of summer flowers in the barn where the caller was giving a big party on Midsummer Day.

'Would you like me to use cottage garden flowers? Lupins, delphiniums, daisies, foxgloves, cornflowers . . . anything that's in bloom at the right time?

I could have them filling the back of the barn in a colourful climbing arrangement of flowers and greenery — and perhaps a sunflower or two somewhere, to celebrate Midsummer Day?'

My caller gasped. 'I can see it already! Sounds quite lovely — and yes to the sunflowers, which will really commemorate the day.'

We discussed terms, and then the call ended. But I thought, as I went into the nursery to see what work was needed, that perhaps the schoolchildren might be allowed to go to this midsummer party — I knew that to see their flowers being used should make them feel very happy and encouraged. A thought I put to the back of my mind, and decided to bring it out at the right time.

Ned came up to me at coffee time, and looked at me very keenly. 'Sorry about Mr Ben leaving,' he said. 'He were a good man. Knew his business about those exotic plants — the customers will miss him and all his knowledge. So you'll have to learn about them in his place, won't you, Miss Rachel?'

I put my empty mug on the table and thought for a moment. He was right, of course. Another task which I must somehow accomplish. Becoming knowledgeable in exotics? And then I smiled to myself. Great-Aunt Georgina would be pleased to have a distant niece learning about her favourite plants. I would start reading a few books this evening.

But a phone call during the busy afternoon called me back from the far summer border where a customer was placing a large order, and I had to make excuses for leaving him, asking Ned to take my place as I went into the office.

'Hi!' said an unknown voice. 'Is that Rachel Swann?'

'Yes . . . ' *Who on earth is it?* I wondered. No one I knew.

'Peter Granger here, judge of the 'Handsome and Out of the Ordinary' prize competition. Rachel, I have great news for you . . . '

I gasped. Why couldn't he just come out with it, whatever it might be? 'Yes?'

I said again, my voice rising shrilly.

The shortest pause, and then, 'Are you sitting down? You need to, because you've won the prize,' he said simply.

Another, longer gasp, and finally I managed to say, 'Are you sure?' That made him laugh, and helped release my emotions. I laughed, too. Then: 'I don't believe you,' I said rudely, trying to catch my breath; but he went on laughing, and then said, more quietly, 'You must believe me, Rachel, because my fellow judges and I had no problem in choosing your arrangement as the winner. It caught the eye with its wild structure and natural colours — and then, of course, that fantastic Bird of Paradise flower at the top just clinched the deal.'

I relaxed in my hard chair and began to smile. I had won the prize! But really it was Ben's gift of his flower which had done it. How I wished he was here to share this amazing news.

'Well, thank you very much, Peter. I'm surprised — but, of course, delighted. So, what's the next step? Do

I have to come up to London to get the award?' I did hope not — we were far too busy for me to take more time off, I thought anxiously.

'Oh no, we'll come down to you. In fact, I'm setting up a few moments on TV of you receiving the prize. I understand you run the family nursery in a Devon village? Well, that should attract viewers. So, would a few minutes of fame please you?'

Fame. I didn't want it, but it had to come, and it would please so many people. Uncle Dexter, Rosemary, Ned and Katie — and those schoolchildren who were part of the nursery now.

And Ben? But he wasn't here, so I pushed that thought away.

'Yes,' I said, with a ring of joy in my voice. 'It sounds wonderful. Just let me know when all this will happen — I must make sure I look the prizewinning part, mustn't I?'

'No,' said Peter quietly. 'Just be yourself, a working gardener with a big talent for arranging flowers. That's what people will want to see.'

And so it was arranged.

Of course, there was enormous excitement when I told everybody. Ned looked a bit doubtful, and said, *What, all those weeds won the prize?* But I laughed and told him that weeds were only beautiful plants in the wrong places. I heard his *Huh!* as he clumped off on to the next job, but at least he was smiling.

When I told Uncle Dexter and Rosemary, there was a silence — in which I sensed a bit of surprise, but mostly pride and pleasure. Uncle's eyes twinkled at me, and he said slowly, 'So you're going to be a television celebrity? That'll do the nursery a lot of good, Rachel. And I shall make sure I'm there —' He looked up at Rosemary. 'We've just been talking about me getting a mobility scooter — what do you think?'

'A marvellous idea, Uncle! Then you can come and oversee us working when all the fuss is over!'

During the weeks ahead, I had messages of congratulations from so many people — Mrs Howarth Jones; the lady whose new commission I would be designing for Midsummer Day; and even Teddy Walters and Bryony, who said the schoolchildren were thrilled and wanted to be there when the TV cameras came to the nursery — would that be possible?

When the great day came, everyone was there: Uncle on his new scooter with Rosemary beside him; Ned and Katie; all my friends and workmates — including the noisy, excited children from school. However, no Ben. I had thought hard about trying to contact him for I knew that this prize had been possible purely with the addition of his wonderful flower. But I had no idea where he was — he could even be in Russia already, I thought wretchedly.

I managed to smile happily as the award was made — the prize a small original painting of a beautiful botanic flower, which I knew would hang in my bedroom forever; and a cheque for a large amount of money, some of which I promised myself would go to Teddy for the school garden.

Although I didn't dress for the occasion, I made sure my hair gleamed, my jeans were clean, and my fingernails not full of brown earth. Peter Granger was a pleasant young man, and the TV camera team were friendly and helpful. 'Stand over there, please, Rachel. No, don't fidget around — just keep still and smile at us. That's it!'

The ordeal was soon over, but I saw Uncle Dexter and Ned talking happily to one of the journalists who was reporting the occasion. He was shown the exotics bed and the school garden, and even had a word with Gareth about growing runner beans. *How lovely*, I thought, *everyone is enjoying themselves. But, oh, how I miss Ben.*

Then it was over, all the packing-up done, and suddenly the nursery was empty of people, save ourselves and a few locals who had come to share the fame.

'A cup of tea, I think,' said Katie, returning to the kitchen, and Ned came up to me, his faded eyes bright and his voice warm. 'You did well, Miss Rachel, and it's wonderful to see your uncle here, and looking so much better. On a scooter, eh? Well, even with bad legs, that means he can still sit in the office, doesn't it?'

'Why, yes, Ned.' I hadn't thought about that, but of course it could happen. Uncle back at work while I did the outside stuff. Yes, it might be the answer to his problems. And I would still be the manager of the nursery.

I went to bed with my head spinning and my eyes already half-closed with weariness. Quickly, I fell into a restorative sleep. Until something woke me.

A tap on the window. What sounded like a handful of gravel thrown up at the panes. I got up, slipped into my robe, and went to look out of the window. The night was dark, and I saw nothing, but I heard a voice. The voice I knew now that I had been waiting to hear, and would always long for. Ben's voice.

'Rachel? Rachel, come down, I want to talk to you.'

I started to say silly things like, *But it's night-time*, and *I thought you were in Russia*, and *Why are you here? What do you want?*

And then I knew everything as he said — in that warm, musical voice — 'Rachel, my love, come down — please come down.'

Rachel, my love. That was enough. I flew downstairs like a chased cat, opened the door — hoping it wouldn't make its usual squeak and wake Katie — and there he was. A tall, dark figure waiting for me outside, backpack thrown onto the far end of the terrace, and his eyes fixed on my face as I ran into his arms.

We didn't speak. Why speak when everything was there in the warmth of his body holding mine?

His lips were gentle at first, slowly growing more demanding; his hand warmed my back; his very presence returned me to a world I had been trying to forget. Ben loved me. And I loved him. Everything was wonderful.

Eventually, we wandered down through

the fragrant gardens to the end of the nursery, where, in shadows, we sat on the old bench beneath the white rose, and talked and talked.

'I saw you on the telly. You were so lovely, and everybody was there in the nursery — only me away. And I knew then that I couldn't possibly go adventuring again, when all I wanted was to be here — with you and the garden.'

I pressed close to him, murmuring, 'And your beloved exotics . . . '

I felt him chuckling. 'But after seeing the Bird of Paradise, you have to admit they're very beautiful.'

'I give in — yes, I might grow to love them.'

We sat there until the first pale colour in the eastern sky told us it was a new day. We stood up, and Ben held me fast in his arms. 'You must go back to bed. You need to sleep after all the excitement of the last few days. But Rachel, my darling Rachel, just let me ask you a question.'

I smiled. He was right — I knew I

would just fall into bed and sleep happily, for my dreams had come true. We were together.

'Yes?' I said, and then opened my eyes wide.

'I want us to get married, my darling. Just say yes, and that's all that matters. And then you can go to bed . . . '

I would never sleep now!

I said, 'Yes, please — as soon as you like . . . ' and then we were kissing again. Close together. *Never to be apart again*, I told myself, and smiled and smiled.

But somehow, a bit later on, we wandered back to the cottage, and I went inside and shut the door on him. He said he would make a bed in the greenhouse — so I left him to it, knowing that this was the last bit of adventuring he would ever do.

We met early in the morning, and agreed we must call on Uncle Dexter and Rosemary and tell them the wonderful news. I imagined Ned had already worked out what had happened, as he grinned all over his face when he saw us together, and said gruffly, 'Good to have you back, Mr Ben. Don't go off again, will you?' before collecting his spade and going off to do some important planting.

Uncle Dexter was having breakfast on the terrace with Rosemary, and looked up in surprise when we arrived. 'That was a short expedition,' he said wryly, grinning at Ben.

Ben held my hand. 'I discovered at the last minute that there was something else — far more important — waiting to be done, sir.'

'I see,' said Uncle, and I knew that he did indeed understand.

But Ben hadn't finished. 'I've asked Rachel to marry me — I should have come to you first, Mr Swann, but she's said yes, and so I hope you agree.'

'My boy, it's the one dream I've been cherishing; but I didn't think it would come true when you went off. Well, now you have my blessing, and I couldn't be more pleased. Come here, Rachel child, and let me give you a kiss.'

Happily, we all embraced, and then Rosemary said, 'I'll make some fresh coffee. I think we all need to get back to reality, don't we?'

We were a laughing, happy little party, sitting there in the early morning sunshine, until Ben said, 'Time for work, Rachel. Let's go.'

'Wait a minute,' Uncle said. 'Just let me add that I shall give you a wedding present of the complete management of Swann Nursery. Between you two, the business can go on — I'll be around if advice is needed, but I won't interfere. Right, so that's all — off you go!'

Back in the nursery we parted: Ben to his exotics bed, and me to the general daily task of weeding, feeding and watering. And soon the customers came, so we were busy all day.

But lunchtime in the cottage, with a smiling Katie making a cake — a special one, she said, to celebrate the good news — we decided a party was important.

'Something small and intimate,' I

said. 'Just us and the family and the nursery people. Let's plan it, Ben, shall we?'

So we planned our wedding party. And I was thrilled when Ben presented me with a beautifully-framed print of my prizewinning flower arrangement. He said, 'This must go in the office, my love — beside your Great-Aunt Georgina. Two Swann people whom future generations will admire and never forget.'

My eyes swam as I envisioned my work up there beside my amazing Great-Aunt, and I knew humbly then that life had given me a present I would always be grateful for.

We were married in the village church, amid flowers and rice and happy smiles and good wishes, and went back to the nursery for the tea party. I was standing by the table which had been laid on the terrace, knife in hand to cut Katie's gorgeous cream-filled cake, with Ben beside me, when something rattled over the entrance gravel. We both looked up, and there was Uncle Dexter, Rosemary at his side, on his mobility scooter.

He came up to us, grinning widely. 'Well,' he said, 'this seems like the end of the family fairy tale, doesn't it? The happy ending we all wanted.'

Ben put his arm around me, drew me close, and gave me a secret smile. And I told myself that Uncle was right, but perhaps another story started here.

We do hope that you have enjoyed reading this large print book.

Did you know that all of our titles are available for purchase?

We publish a wide range of high quality large print books including:
Romances, Mysteries, Classics
General Fiction
Non Fiction and Westerns

Special interest titles available in large print are:
The Little Oxford Dictionary
Music Book, Song Book
Hymn Book, Service Book

Also available from us courtesy of Oxford University Press:
Young Readers' Dictionary
(large print edition)
Young Readers' Thesaurus
(large print edition)

For further information or a free brochure, please contact us at:
Ulverscroft Large Print Books Ltd.,
The Green, Bradgate Road, Anstey,
Leicester, LE7 7FU, England.
Tel: (00 44) 0116 236 4325
Fax: (00 44) 0116 234 0205

CHRISTMAS REVELATIONS

Jill Barry

Reluctant 1920s debutante Annabel prefers horses to suitors. When she tumbles into the path of Lawrence, Lord Lassiter, she's annoyed that this attractive man is the despised thirteenth guest joining her family for Christmas — for he has been involved in a recent scandal, and only he and his faithful valet, Norman Bassett, know the truth behind the gossip. Meanwhile, as Lawrence tries to charm Annabel, Norman has a surprise encounter with a figure from his past — one who has been keeping a secret from him for years . . .

WHERE THE HEART LIES

Sheila Spencer-Smith

Amy sets off to join her wildlife photographer boyfriend Mark on the Isles of Scilly, accompanied by her sister's dog Rufus, who she is dropping off with her sister's parents-in-law, Jim and Maria, at Penmarrow Caravan Site. But when she arrives, the park is deserted — except for the handsome Callum Savernack, who doesn't appear happy to have her there. When it emerges that Jim and Maria are temporarily unable to return to Penmarrow, Amy finds herself torn between her responsibilities to Mark, to Rufus — and to Callum . . .